# Paradise Disguised
## Passion in Paradise, Texas

Liliana Hart

Copyright © 2011 Liliana Hart

All rights reserved.

ISBN: 1467971979
ISBN-13: 978-1467971973

# CONTENTS

| | |
|---|---|
| Chapter One | 1 |
| Chapter Two | 17 |
| Chapter Three | 30 |
| Chapter Four | 45 |
| Chapter Five | 60 |
| Chapter Six | 75 |
| Chapter Seven | 87 |
| Chapter Eight | 103 |
| Chapter Nine | 112 |
| Chapter Ten | 125 |
| Chapter Eleven | 146 |
| Chapter Twelve | 155 |
| Chapter Thirteen | 170 |
| Chapter Fourteen | 181 |
| Chapter Fifteen | 196 |
| Epilogue | 201 |

# CHAPTER ONE

Anna Hollis stood frozen as she watched her dream man walk by, utterly oblivious to her existence on the planet. She wanted him in a way that was completely at odds with her usual shyness and cautiously stole another glance in his direction. From his dark hair with the sun bleached tips that curled slightly over his collar to his hard, lean body. A working man's body, with rough callused hands and muscles in all the right places.

His eyes were a silvery shade of blue and the one time they had made eye contact, she thought she'd pass out from their intensity. Everything about him made her body tingle in areas she never thought possible.

She pushed her glasses up higher on the bridge of her nose and continued stocking the circular saws that had just arrived early that morning. Every box in the store sported a label she was proud of.

*Hollis Tools: Three Generations Built to Last.*

Her grandfather had started making his own tools sixty years ago, and what had started as a hobby to the wealthy banker, quickly became an enterprise so large that he'd had to open a hardware store to get rid of some of them.

Her dream man had been coming in the store for months, and she'd been lusting after him since the first moment she'd laid eyes on him. Not that he'd noticed. Nobody noticed her.

He was at the checkout counter talking to her father, and she only drooled a little at the way his backside fit into a worn pair of Levi's. There was a small hole in the corner of the pocket, and if she stared hard enough she was pretty sure she could see skin.

Her imagination went into overdrive as she pictured herself sitting on the counter, his muscled body thrusting eagerly between her spread thighs. Hell, she'd pictured them making love in every part of the store. She never knew there were so many creative ideas hidden inside her mind.

Her cheeks heated as she saw her father glance over the man's shoulder, probably wondering what she could be thinking about that caused her to have hot flashes on a busy Saturday morning.

She jerked herself back to reality, disappointed to

hear the bells jingle above the door that signaled his departure. She was already looking forward to his visit next week.

Anna sighed wistfully and went back to stocking the saws. The smell of fresh cut lumber and saw dust enveloped her in a comforting embrace, a bouquet she'd grown up with and learned to love. It blended well with the spicy scent of her dream man.

She was in sad, sad shape. Ever since he'd walked through the door, all she could think about was sex. She'd had sex—once—but by the way her body was tingling now she knew it hadn't been done right.

She was twenty-five years old for God's sake, and she read romance novels. What she had experienced that one night had not even come close to satisfying her expectations. Most people her age were married and just starting their families, but she was still looking for basic chemistry and mind blowing sex. And boy did she have chemistry with the mystery man. Of course, that didn't mean he had it with her.

She was completely unappealing as a woman, and it was her own fault. Not even the fact that she was an heiress to a multi-million dollar company convinced men to ask her out. She was painfully shy, which explained why she only had one close friend and few acquaintances. And that was an almost impossible fete in a town the size of Paradise. She'd neglected her looks to keep attention on anything but herself. She was wallpaper, and she liked it that way. Most of the time.

Of course, every time her dream man walked in she wanted to rip off all of her clothes and display herself like a turkey dinner at Thanksgiving amidst all the power tools. Her nipples tightened painfully under her flannel shirt, and she breathed slowly to get herself under control.

She had to do something if she wanted to have the wild night she'd been dreaming about. She had style. She knew how to dress to her advantage and apply the right makeup. It was something her mother had excelled at and taught her daughter to use to her own advantage.

Anna had been outgoing as a teenager, popular in school, and she'd always had all the right clothes. But then her mother had died.

Her dark brown hair was long, almost to her waist, and she kept it in a long thick braid down the center of her back. It was a good color and texture—she just never bothered to do much with it. She never wore makeup and she wore dark framed glasses to cover her startling turquoise eyes. It was time some changes were made.

She had no desire to get married or have a family. She wouldn't be able to bear it if she lost someone else she loved, and the best way of avoiding that was to keep her distance from any serious relationships. But the one thing she did want with all her heart was one crazy night with her dream man. And she was going to do everything in her power to see she got it.

*God . . . What if he was married?* That would ruin everything.

"Why don't you take the rest of the day off?"

The sound of her father's voice snapped her back to reality. She turned and smiled at him, knowing she could never have asked for a better man for a father. They'd raised each other since her mother's death ten years before.

Her father had worked hard to expand Hollis Tools from the small hardware store her grandfather had started to a multi-million dollar enterprise with dozens of stores all over Texas. Their goal was to expand nationwide in the next ten years. And you could always find a Hollis working in their flagship store in Paradise, Texas. They knew the business inside and out.

"Why would I want to take a day off on the busiest day of the week?" She asked, grinning, the dimple in her left cheek a stunning reminder of her mother.

"I've been thinking that you've been spending too much time in the store lately. You never go out and visit your friends, and when you're not here, you're at home with one of your books."

"I'm here because I like to be here," she said.

"Do you know the man that was just in here?" her father asked.

Anna blushed at the mention of her dream man. Surely her father didn't suspect the erotic visions that had played through her mind every time he entered the store.

"N...No," she stuttered, looking at his chest instead of his eyes. "Should I know him?"

"You've probably heard of him," he said. "That was Dylan Maguire."

"You mean *the* Dylan Maguire of Maguire Homes?" Anna asked tentatively. Maguire Homes was the best in the business. Every job got the owner's personal attention, from drawing up the plans to the last brick set in place. Now she had a name to add to her fantasies, and it put a small hitch in her fantasies. Dylan Maguire was not exactly low profile. But he sure was fine to look at. It might be worth it, she thought. Anna blanked out momentarily at the thought of screaming his name in passion.

"That's the one. He told me that he's starting to have some breathing room in his schedule. I thought you might like to pay him a visit and see about building your own place."

Anna was a little hurt that her father wanted her to move out. They'd shared the Hollis mansion for many years, just the two of them, and she couldn't imagine living anywhere else.

"I don't know, dad." She did get lonely at times. The only company they ever saw was the household staff or her best friend Mel. "I like the seclusion our house provides." That wasn't always necessarily true, but she told herself she enjoyed the solitude to ease the occasional ache she felt deep within her breast.

"Anna, you need to do this for yourself. You're mother's been gone a long time, and she wouldn't want to see you living the way you are now. You act as if you've already got one foot in the grave, when you have an entire lifetime ahead of you."

"Well . . . If that's what you want I can make an appointment with him for next week," Anna said, hurt more than she wanted to admit at her father's rejection.

"No, of course it's not what I want," Jack answered. "I'd love for you to stay under the same roof with me until my last days, but I'm thinking this is something you should do for yourself. Don't feel like I'm trying to get rid of you. Think of it as a gentle nudge out of the nest. You've got money. Why don't you go a little crazy and spend some of it? Go shopping, and do all those things that other women do. Get a place of your own, and stay out all hours of the night. I just want you to be happy," he said. "You're a young woman, not an old geezer like me."

"I am happy, dad, and you know I love you very much. And besides, you're not that old. I never see you go out and live it up on the weekends either."

"Yes, but I'm set in my ways," he told her affectionately. "Why don't you put that business degree to some use? There's no need for you to come into the store every day. You've been running the business behind the scenes for years anyway. You can work out of your own office, and you'll get the chance to travel and see how all your hard work is paying off at the other stores. I want you to have more freedom."

Anna thought about what he'd said and knew he was right. Hell, it was what she'd been thinking before he'd mentioned it. It was the perfect time to make some changes in her boring life.

"You're right, dad. It's time I made some drastic changes to my life. I don't know why I haven't done it before now," she said, taking off her work gloves and laying them on the shelf half-way filled with power saws. She enjoyed working in the store because it was an easy way to be apart of small town life, without actually being a part of it.

"That's my girl," he said with relief. "I was hoping you'd at least give it a try. If you hate it, there will always be room with me."

Anna gave her father another hug, but her mind was already thinking of the future. "Can you get our attorney to purchase some property in the area? And have him call Mr. Maguire and set up an appointment for two weeks from Monday. That should be plenty of time for the new me to be presentable."

"Why don't you give Mel a call? I bet she'd like to be a part of the new you, too."

Anna thought of her childhood friend and smiled. Amelia James, was called Mel by everyone except her own mother, and she was Anna's complete opposite. She had a bubbly and outgoing personality that drew in anyone around her and a witty sarcasm that could cut people off at the knees without them knowing it.

She was petite and willowy next to Anna's more statuesque figure and she was in constant motion. Anna realized she'd like Mel's company very much. She'd neglected her friends like she'd neglected herself, but that was about to change as well.

Dylan Maguire sat at his desk and thought about the sexy brunette he saw every week at *Hollis Tools*. She had a great body that she kept hidden under layers of clothing. The only reason he'd found out the secret of her curvaceous figure was because he couldn't take his eyes off of her when he was in the store, and he'd just happened to catch denim and cotton stretch in strategic places as she reached up to a shelf.

He'd made a stop by the hardware store at least once a week for months to get a glimpse of that sexy body she tried so hard to hide. He'd have to be a saint not to notice a body like hers, lush and round just the way a woman should be. And everybody knew that Dylan Maguire was no saint. He genuinely appreciated all facets of a woman, whether they were twenty or one-hundred twenty, thin or plump, homely or beautiful, they were just fascinating creatures. Of course, one that was twenty might hold his attention for a different reason.

Sometimes he had to make up excuses to stop in *Hollis Tools*, but it was always worth the trip. He also stopped by for the useful pieces of information he was able to get out of Jack Hollis. Dylan knew the girl was Jack's daughter and that she'd been extremely withdrawn since her mother's death. He also knew Jack was trying to get her to come out of her shell.

Dylan had casually mentioned he was in the middle of his slow season—though the truth was the opposite—just to see if Jack would tell him some more information about Anna. He'd hit a gold mine.

Jack had come up with the idea of Anna getting out on her own, and he thought Dylan was just the person to help her out. Jack would probably have changed his mind if he'd known the only thing he wanted to help Anna out of was her clothes and a good bit of her innocence.

The woman had a body that wouldn't quit, and she'd caused him plenty of uncomfortable nights since he'd first set eyes on her several months ago. Anna was a natural beauty, and there was nothing she could do to hide the fact. He'd spent many a night fantasizing about what it would be like to unravel her braid slowly and run his fingers through her thick hair. He could imagine it curly and untamed, spread out on her pillow as he made love to her gently, and he could imagine it wrapped around his fist as he took her from behind with harsh, fast strokes.

He'd take those horrid glasses off her face that hid the most beautiful eyes he'd ever seen and throw them in the trash. He'd seen her staring at him one too many times out of the corner of his eye, and he also knew she was just as attracted to him as he was to her. All he had to do was walk by to feel the sexual tension crackling through the air, and his cock automatically hardened every time he imagined stripping away those layers of clothes she wore like a shield..

His sexual appetite could be voracious at times, and he knew that Anna's shyness could be a problem. But God. . . he hoped she was open to a little adventure. It had been too long since he'd been truly satisfied by a woman.

He heard two knocks before his architect and best friend, Mitchell Casey, walked through the door.

"Whoa buddy, from the scowl on your face am I to assume you're having woman trouble?" Mitchell said, good-naturedly.

"No, you're the only annoyance I'm seeing right

now," Dylan said.

"Well, from the size of the boner you're sporting, consider me flattered."

Mitchell just laughed at the obscene gesture Dylan shot him and sat down in the empty chair in front of the desk. "So who's the lucky lady this time?"

"I'm not saying a word," Dylan said adamantly. "I haven't even had a conversation with her yet."

"Ahh . . . Lust at first sight. My favorite."

"You're a degenerate. No wonder you have a hard time finding a date," Dylan said, even though he knew women were practically taking numbers to go out with *The* Mitchell Casey. He was the ultimate love-em'-and-leave-em' man.

The two of them had become friends in college, and they'd been working together ever since. Mitchell had helped him through his divorce several years ago, and he had helped Mitchell survive after the death of his wife.

Of course, Mitchell had turned into a hardened, cynical man, and it was obvious to everyone but Mitchell that he went through women like water to drown out the pain that was still smothering him. They owed each other a great deal, and they'd decided the best place to start anew was Paradise, Texas. What could be better than that?

The buzz on the intercom brought his thoughts and body under control as he reminded himself that he was at work. His secretary buzzed a second time, and he picked up the receiver ready to get back to the grindstone.

"Yes, Janet," he said.

"Mr. Hollis is on line one. He said that he'd talked to you earlier about building a house for his daughter," Janet said, curious as always.

"I'll take the call on my private line," he said, knowing that would pique her interest even more. He couldn't help having a perverse sense of humor.

Janet Porter was in her early thirties and reminded him of a modern day pin-up girl from the forties. She had bleached blonde hair, a curvy figure and a kewpie doll mouth she kept painted bright red. She was more cute than anything, and he'd always been surprised he'd never been attracted to her, but he knew she was the one that kept the office running smoothly. They'd eventually become friends, and he was satisfied to leave it that way.

"Aha. Jack Hollis. That explains everything," Mitchell said. "The only place you've been today is to Hollis Tools, and I know just the brunette who could put that look on your face. I've never thought much of her face or the frumpy clothes, but she does have the type of body that could make a man crawl."

Dylan looked at Mitchell sharply, warning him with a

glance that he'd better stay clear of Anna. "And how would you know anything about her body," Dylan growled.

"I'm a professional observer of all women. Believe me, I know what a woman looks like without her clothes on no matter how much she tries to hide. But don't worry, my friend, I've looked, but she's not my type," Mitchell assured him with a dimpled grin. "I like my women with a little more flash."

Dylan shooed a laughing Mitchell out of the office and answered the phone.

"Mr. Hollis?" Dylan asked.

"Call me Jack, son. I'm glad I caught you in the office. I've talked to Anna, and she's agreed to meet with you and get started on a new place of her own. I thought she'd put up more of a fight, but I hardly had to prod her at all."

He worked fast, Dylan thought to himself. Either that or Anna was more anxious to meet him than he'd thought. Boy how he'd love to be the one to break her of her shyness. He had a whole new world to introduce her to.

"I've had a nice piece of property tucked away that I bought some years ago. It would be the perfect spot for Anna. It's full of trees and a little creek runs along the property line. I'm going to sign it over to her as a surprise."

"That sounds great. When does she want to meet?" Dylan asked, already anticipating the visit.

"She said make it two weeks from Monday," Jack said.

Dylan deflated in disappointment at the delayed meeting. Maybe she wasn't as excited to meet him as he thought.

Jack went on to explain the circumstances. "I think the little talk I had with her caused her to have a breakthrough. She said she's ready to turn over a new leaf and start a new life. I can't wait to see how it turns out, but she wanted the two weeks to get things in order before you meet. She's always been a treasure, and I want this to work out for her. She deserves it."

"I'll do the best I can to make sure she gets everything she wants," Dylan said, heartened by Jack's words. He couldn't wait to meet the new Anna either, and he'd make sure he was part of her new life.

"All I ask as that you take care of my little girl and make her happy," Jack said before hanging up.

"Oh, believe me, sir, I will," Dylan said to an empty line.

Jack Hollis hung up the phone a very happy man. Young people were so gullible these days. Dylan and Anna must think him the dumbest man on the planet to not feel the sparks that flew between them every time they were in the same room. Their chemistry was practically electric.

Dylan Maguire didn't look like a man to let a good opportunity pass him by, and Anna was a late bloomer just like her mother had been. She just needed a little encouragement to grow. He knew her shyness was a result of her mother's death. It was the only way she could protect herself from the pain of the loss. Hell, she'd only had him as an example, and he'd been doing the same thing. It was all his fault, and he'd do anything to repair the damage that had already been done. There was still a chance for his baby.

Anna was ready to be swept off her feet, and in his opinion, it was high time Dylan settled down with a good woman. A man past thirty needed a woman to help settle his wild ways. They were a perfect match and both were primed for the pickings.

He thought of his wife and knew she'd skin him alive for messing with their only daughter's future. But he had a good feeling about those two. "You'll see, sweetheart," he said looking towards the sky. "Everything will work out all right."

## CHAPTER TWO

Anna drove her sensible Volvo down Baker Street, smack dab in the middle of Paradise—population 3,231.

The Baker sisters had been prostitutes in the late part of the nineteenth century, and apparently they'd been popular enough to warrant having the main street in town named after them. The more she thought about it, maybe the Baker sisters were the reason the town was called Paradise.

The two-story Victorian house where they'd run their business still sat on the corner of the Towne Square, only now it was used as a bed and breakfast. Anna always felt the town trivia added character to an otherwise unremarkable place.

She waved to a couple of familiar people along the busy cobblestone street and waited while pedestrians crossed back and forth, unmindful of the no jay-walking signs posted.

Mr. Larson and Mr. Duffy played checkers on the wooden walkway in front of Howard's Grocery, and a mother held the hands of her two small children and led them into the ice cream parlor. Everything was just as it always had been, and Anna couldn't imagine living anywhere else. It really was paradise.

*Hollis Tools* was on the corner of the opposite street and brought in business from the other towns close by. It had helped Paradise survive during many a hard time by employing as many local workers as possible. The other stores and restaurants on the street lined up, straight as soldiers, next to it. It was a town rich with tradition, and hardly anyone was a stranger in such a small place. Unless they stayed secluded from everyone like she had attempted to over the past ten years.

Anna maneuvered her Volvo around the corner and through the Towne Square, and then headed in a straight shot towards Mel's house. The Volvo was going to be a thing of the past. She needed a new car to fit with her new image, something sexy and sleek. Of course, she didn't have a new image yet. She was still wearing the same baggy clothes and tight braid she always wore, but she'd changed on the inside.

Mel's house was located in Paradise's historic district, right across from a large park, full of trees, a jogging path and playground toys.

Mel had taken over her family's bookstore after she'd graduated from college, and she'd promptly added a café to one side of it to attract more customers. It was a homey place where you could end up staying for hours. Fortunately, Mel was off on Sundays, and she'd agreed to help a friend in need.

Anna hadn't told Mel the real reason behind her change. She didn't know how her friend would react if she found out she only wanted to quench this sexual need that consumed her body. Two weeks seemed like an eternity, and that was if Dylan was even interested.

She beeped the horn, and Mel came bounding out of the house, her shoulder bag hanging over her arm, as energetic as ever. Anna envied Mel's original style. Her jeans had holes in both knees, and she wore a long-sleeved t-shirt that was just short enough to show off her bellybutton ring.

*Maybe I should get a bellybutton ring.*

"I'm so glad you called me," Mel said, slamming the car door shut and putting on a pair of aviator sunglasses. "It's been too long since we've gotten together."

"I want to apologize for that," Anna said. "I haven't been a very good friend, but I'd like to change that. If you don't mind?"

"Of course I don't mind. We've been friends our whole lives, why should that change now?" Mel asked, shaking her head at the silliness of it all. "Now let's stop all this mushy talk. I want to know the real reason for this change you're so insistent on. It's a man isn't it?"

Anna took a deep breath and decided to go for the truth. "There's this man that's been coming into the store for months . . ."

"I knew it, I knew it had to be a man," Mel interrupted. "What does he look like? Is he hot?"

"Well, if you'll let me finish I'll tell you," Anna said, exasperated.

"Sorry, but don't leave out anything," Mel said, unfazed.

"I can't even begin to describe what looking at this man does to my body. He's really tall, probably 6'5", and he has this amazing body that's muscled in all the right places. He's got dark hair that never seems to be tamed. It always curls a little bit around the collar, and God. . . his eyes are this silvery blue that just captivate me with one glance. He's just so . . . so full of testosterone and heat."

"Geez . . . Now I'm having hot flashes," Mel murmured in reverence.

"I'm going to do everything in my power to make him notice me," Anna said.

"I don't think it will be as hard as you think. You've always underestimated your looks. All we need to do is punch them up a little bit."

"Speaking of that, where are we going first?"

"I made an appointment for you with my hairdresser at *DeLucia's*."

"But you usually have to book weeks in advance," Anna said as worry of what she was about to undertake creased her brow.

"Well, she slipped you into her schedule as a favor. Plus, I told her you had loads of money and would make it worth her while."

"Thanks," Anna said wryly, raising her eyebrow in exasperation.

Mel's cropped locks caused a small niggling of doubt enter her mind. Mel changed her hair like it was day of the week underpants. Right now, her dark hair was short and managed to stick up in every direction, but look stylish and chic at the same time. She'd also had some blonde highlights put in since the last time they'd seen each other. "Are you sure she'll do a good job?" Anna asked tentatively.

"Oh yeah, she's the best."

They were headed to Fort Worth, the closest city, because as much as she loved Paradise, it wasn't the place to reinvent herself. She wouldn't let Della at *Della's Salon* do her hair for any amount of money in the world. If she wanted gossip, then that's where she'd go, but never for a hairstyle unless she wanted to end up with blue tinted poodle curls like every other senior citizen in the town.

Anna pulled into the parking lot of *De Lucia's Spa and Salon* and felt a little better. The sign wasn't in neon, and people weren't running out the front door screaming, so she guessed it was safe. It didn't look like a place that appealed to punk rockers despite Mel's hair.

Anna dragged her feet, nervous for the first time since she'd gotten the hair-brained idea to reinvent herself in her head. What had she been thinking? She'd let her hormones do the thinking, that was the problem.

"Geez, Anna. You're not going to the firing squad, and they only poke hot sticks in your eyes if you wear last season's wardrobe."

"What?" Anna squeaked.

"Relax. I'm kidding. I don't think you're wearing clothes from this millennia, so they'll probably take pity on you." Mel grabbed Anna's arm and pulled her through the doors.

"Good morning, Mel," the young man behind the counter said.

"Hi, Paul. Are they all ready for us?"

Paul was a thin man dressed in all black with thick Buddy Holly glasses, and the most awesome shade of pink nail polish was painted on his manicured nails.

"Us?" Anna asked curiously.

"I'm going to get a facial and a massage while you're getting you hair done. Then we'll go eat lunch some place that serves calories. All they give you here is wheat germ and bean sprouts," Mel said in a whisper. "But they have great champagne."

"It's nine o'clock in the morning!" Anna said, scandalized by the thought.

"I thought you were turning over a new leaf," Mel said.

"Maybe I'll have a mimosa," Anna said. "That doesn't count does it?"

"That's my girl. Now go get styled, and I'll meet you back out here in a little while."

Anna watched Mel disappear down a long corridor, and she was left all alone with Paul.

He gave her a reassuring smile. "You're in very good hands. You'll be a new woman before you know it. It must be one amazing man to make you want to do all of this."

"Oh, he's definitely worth it. I've been waiting a long time to feel like this. I'm a little out of the loop, but Mel told me good men with health insurance and all their teeth are hard to find."

"Honey, don't I know it," Paul said, winking. He led her down the opposite corridor from Mel, and they ended up at the far end of the hall. "You're going to be with Jessica. She's really talented. You'll like her."

Jessica came out to greet her, and Anna almost fainted at the sight of the woman with the shaved head. There was a hawk tattooed on the top of her skull, and her nose and eyebrows had hoops in them.

"I hear we're doing an overhaul," Jessica said.

"Y...Yes." Anna mentally kicked herself for stuttering. It was something she hadn't started doing until twenty-four hours ago.

"Cool glasses. Do you have to wear them to see?" Jessica asked lifting the glasses off Anna's face.

"No, they're only a light prescription. I . . ." Anna stood flabbergasted as Jessica snapped her glasses right in two.

"They didn't fit with your new image," she explained.

"Oh," Anna said as she held the two broken pieces in her hands.

"Can I get you something to drink before you get started," Paul asked.

"I'll take a mimosa. And keep em' coming," Anna said, prepared to drink her fears away.

Mel dressed in the privacy of one of the dressing rooms, her body relaxed and limber after the massage she'd just received. She couldn't wait to see Anna. It was long overdue in her opinion.

Mel remembered what Anna was like before her mother's death. The two of them had been peas in a pod, getting into mischief and talking about boys. But Anna had withdrawn after Mrs. Hollis died. They'd still been friends, but there was always something missing. Mel could already see a difference in Anna in the short time they'd been together that morning. She'd have to find the man that was having this effect on her and shake his hand. Now if she could only find her own man, she'd be all set. Maybe Anna's dream man had a brother.

Mel waited in the lobby impatiently, pacing back and forth in front of a large fountain.

"Calm down, Mel," Paul said, like a mother hen. "She looks great. But I think you're going to have to feed her soon, because she's had three mimosas."

"You got her drunk?" Mel asked. "Anna's never been

drunk in her life."

"Well, she kept asking for them," Paul said defensively. "Besides, she looked like she needed the extra reinforcement."

Mel was interrupted by the opening door. Anna stood in the center of it, absolutely breathtaking. "Holy shit," Mel muttered.

"Don't you just love it?" Anna asked excitedly, twirling like a ballerina.

Her hair had been highlighted with several shades of dark blonde. It was still the same glorious length it had always been, but Jessica had added layers to lighten up the weight of it slightly. The layers also made it curl riotously down her back. Makeup had been artfully applied to her already beautiful face—enhancing her looks—and her fingernails and toenails were painted bright California Pink, the exact shade that Paul's were.

"You look amazing," Mel said.

"I know, can you believe it?" Anna said, without any modesty at all. "My toes are so sexy."

"Yes, but the flannel shirt and jeans have to go. You passed the grunge stage in the Nineties."

"Well let's go shopping then," Anna said, slurring her words only a little.

"Why don't we get some lunch first, tiger? Then we'll hit the mall," Mel said, laughing at Anna's tipsy state.

Anna started to get her wits back after lunch. "I can't believe I drank so much. I have to say, though, that it wasn't an unpleasant feeling. We'll have to do it again. Just not in public next time."

"Well, I hope you've got your credit card handy, because it's going to be smoking pretty soon," Mel said.

Anna was amazed at all the clothes and shoes that filled the stores. And to her surprise, Mel led her to areas that suited Anna well. She thought for sure she'd end up with a closet full of tight t-shirts and hip hugging jeans.

She bought several business suits, since she'd decided to take up her father's offer of working on the owner's side of Hollis Tools instead of spending so much time in the store. She'd get to travel to all of the stores and check on their progress at least a couple of times a year, and any changes that needed to be made would be her decision. She also bought several casual pieces for everyday wear and shoes to go with everything. The beiges and bland colors that currently lived in her closet were about to be things of the past. Her new wardrobe was an explosion of color, and she'd never seen so many boxes in her life.

"Okay . . . I want a pair of those jeans you have on," Anna told Mel.

"Are you sure? They have holes in them."

"I don't know why, but I think those jeans are really sexy," Anna said.

"Well let's go get a couple of pair and then we'll look for lingerie."

Anna was exhausted by the time they made it back to Paradise. She'd never had so much fun in her life. If she couldn't get Dylan's attention now, then nothing would. And the lingerie. . . She'd bought more lingerie than she could possibly use, but she wanted to give Dylan variety, just in case. Of course, she'd need instructions to get some of those contraptions on.

She dropped Mel off at her house, enjoying the tidy neighborhood of older homes. "Thanks for coming with me today," she said as she hugged Mel tightly. "We'll do this again very soon."

"Hell yes, we will," Mel said. "I want to go with you when you buy your new car. I've decided to live vicariously through you. And I really want to meet this man. Just because he's setting off your hormonal alarms doesn't mean he'll pass the Mel test."

Anna laughed at her outrageous friend, glad she'd called her to come with her. She'd missed her more than she realized. "You have nothing to worry about. I thoroughly plan to be the one that uses him. I need the practice. I'm not looking for a long term relationship. I just need to get my lust-hazed brain satisfied so I can focus on other things. This guy is killing me."

Mel was a little surprised by that statement. Anna was not the type of woman to indulge in one night stands, and Mel had a hard time believing that Anna's heart wouldn't become involved once she had a physical relationship with this guy. She had commitment written all over her.

"I just want you to be careful. The heart is not something to trifle with."

"Yes, Maam," Anna said, rolling her eyes as she waved and drove away.

## CHAPTER THREE

Dylan watched out his window as the silver Mercedes convertible pulled into an available parking spot. He was a little surprised. A car like that didn't exactly go with the flannel-clad woman he'd seen at the hardware store.

Her choice of cars made him want her even more. He had a weakness for expensive cars, like the Aston Martin that sat covered in his garage. He'd been working too much lately to enjoy the indulgence of a fast drive in such an incredible machine. His work truck served a functional purpose, but it wasn't exactly a chick magnet.

He'd been ready to combust for the past two weeks, walking around with a permanent hard-on. Anna had filled his dreams with erotic visions and left him wanting like he'd never wanted anyone before.

He'd made extra trips to Hollis Tools over the past two weeks, hoping to get a glimpse of Anna, but she'd been nowhere in sight. Jack had told him she'd taken some time off and wouldn't be spending so much time in the store in the future, but God, how he'd missed not seeing those luminous eyes tracking his whereabouts.

He closed the blinds and sat down at his desk, trying desperately to look like he was doing something besides fantasizing. Normally, he'd have Mitchell sit in on a client's first visit so he could start drawing up plans, but he wanted Anna all to himself.

Janet buzzed him on his office link to let him know of Anna's arrival.

"Anna Hollis to see you," Janet said.

"Send her in please," he said. Anticipation had his hands clasped in a white-knuckled grip on the arm of his chair.

When she walked in, Dylan was entranced by the vivid turquoise eyes that met his gaze. It was like being hit head on by a Mack truck. His cock twitched in anticipation and thickened painfully at the vision that stood in front of him. He exhaled slowly to try and relieve some of the pressure behind his zipper.

*Holy God.* She looked better than even he'd

imagined. He did a slow perusal of her body. The frumpy clothes were gone, replaced with a sleek business suit in "fuck me red." The pencil skirt came modestly just above her knees, but the four-inch heels she wore made her legs look like they went on forever. God how he wanted those shoes around his waist. She wore a matching jacket that zipped up the front, and she had it unzipped about an inch, so a hint of cleavage showed.

"Anna?" He asked, a little in awe. "Wow. I almost didn't recognize you. You've made quite a change since the last time I saw you."

He could tell his words threw her off stride. He was sure she thought she'd gone unnoticed by him and he watched her carefully built confidence crumble slightly. Her show of weakness emboldened him, and he recognized the shy young woman he'd lusted after.

He got up from behind his desk and extended his hand to her in greeting, his erection prominent behind the zipper of his jeans.

Her eyes grew wide at his extended hand and she stuttered a little. "Oh…I…I didn't realize we'd met before."

Anna blushed prettily as her shyness warred with curiosity. She'd left her hand in his and gently rubbed the rough calluses on his fingers, driving him to distraction in the process.

"We've never been formally introduced, but I've noticed you every time I'm in the store. I'm Dylan Maguire."

"Anna Hollis," she said, her hand still trapped by his.

"I'm glad you got rid of the glasses. You have beautiful eyes," he told her.

He almost laughed as she gulped audibly, and he knew his verbal torment was going to be keeping him awake all night.

"Thank you," she said, finally extricating her hand from his. She broke eye contact and walked slowly around his office, giving him the view of a lifetime in the process. She had the roundest ass, and he couldn't wait to get his hands on it.

"What can I help you with today, Anna?" He asked her, returning to the chair behind his desk. "Jack told me you might be interested in building your own place."

"Yes, that's right," she answered. "My dad gave me some land as a gift, and I'd like to build a place of my own as soon as possible. It's just on the border of the original Hollis land, not too far from here. I don't want anything too big, just a comfortable place that I can enjoy for the rest of my life. The trees and the creek will make a good backdrop. I'd like the design of the house to stay true to the land."

"We'll go meet with my architect and see what he can come up with after we're through here. He can help you put all your ideas on paper and then we'll get started making your dreams come true."

She smiled tentatively at him, but Dylan wasn't going to let her go so easy. She'd worked up the courage to change her appearance and meet him face to face, and he was going to make her finish what she started.

"Anna," he said, caressingly. "Tell me why you've really come."

She looked confused and shook her head in denial. "I just told you why I'm here."

"You only told me part of the reason, and I think it was more of an excuse to come here than a reason anyway." He got up and stood close in front of her, their bodies a breath apart. "I want you to tell me the real reason for coming, the reason for changing your appearance. Be honest."

Anna took a big breath and let it out in a rush. The moment of truth was upon her, not only for Dylan but for herself as well. "I wanted you to notice me."

"Oh, I noticed you all right. Why do you think I came in the store so often?" he asked. "My shed is stocked full of more tools than I can possibly use in this lifetime."

Dylan moved closer so the heat of his erection

brushed against her, and he heard her gasp in surprise. Her breathing became heavy and he could see the rise and fall of her breasts with each breath.

"Now tell me the rest, why did you come to me specifically?" He pulled her body closer, so their breaths meshed with every exhale. He skimmed the tip of his fingers down the side of her breasts to her ribs. "Tell me," he demanded.

"I want you to teach me," she blurted out.

"What do you want me to teach you?" he asked. His breath fanned her ear, and he felt the shivers coursing through her body. He inhaled her scent and could smell the musky layer of arousal floating between them.

"I want you to teach me how to be sexy." She worked up her courage and looked him square in the eyes. "I want you to teach me about sex, everything about it. I want to be seen as a woman, and I want you to make my body feel heavy and tingle like it does every time you walk into a room."

Dylan watched her cheeks flush with color and duck her head in embarrassment. He was completely speechless. He'd never met a woman who was so brazen, yet so innocent at the same time. His body was hot enough to self-combust, and she had absolutely no idea the effect she was having on him. He tilted her chin back up with his finger and brought her eyes to meet his.

"You don't need me to teach you how to be sexy. You are so fucking sexy I could come in my jeans just by looking at you." He appreciated the way her pupils dilated at his crude words. "I thought you were sexy before you changed your clothes and your hair. You have a body that every man fantasizes about, and you've been the star of my dreams for months."

"I have?" she whispered.

"Oh yes," Dylan said. "And I had every intention of bringing you out of your shell eventually, but fortunately, you did it on your own. That just means we can move our affair forward, skip all the pleasantries and just get down to the pleasure."

Dylan knew that Anna's lack of experience could work to his advantage. He would get the opportunity to mold and instruct her in the art of passion, something he'd never gotten to do before, as most of his previous partners had been long past experienced. And most importantly, he'd make sure she liked sex just the way he did, hard and fast and dirty, any time and any place. There were few women in this world that could satisfy his sexual appetite, and he was determined to make Anna one of them.

"So you'll teach me?" she asked hesitantly.

Dylan snapped back from his lusty vision and focused on the wide-eyed stare in front of him. "Oh yeah, I'll teach you. And your first lesson is to never be shy or hesitant around me. If you want something, I want you to ask for it. No matter what it is. I'll do my best to give it to you."

Anna still looked unsure at his command, but he admired the way she stuck out her chin and did as he said, even though she was flushed red in embarrassment.

"I want you to kiss me," she said. Her voice only quivered slightly at the request.

Dylan brought her body closer, so she was leaning against him, and he ran his hands down her back slowly until he cradled her ass in his hands. She had such a great backside, full and firm. It fit perfectly in his hands.

He pressed her against his body, closer, closer, until they were heat to heat, her thighs cradling his hardness.

She moaned in anticipation, unknown feelings rioting through her body, and Dylan almost lost control. He wanted nothing more than to devour the sweet mouth in front of him, but self control prevailed…barely. He had to savor this first kiss.

Dylan brought his lips closer and teased her, nipping at her chin and the corners of her mouth. He chuckled at the frustrated sigh she gave, impatient to have his lips join with hers. His eyes were wide open and stared into the fathomless depths of her turquoise orbs. His tongue traced the outline of her lips and she parted them, ready for all of him.

Dylan took the kiss slowly, deepening it with a gentle thrust of his tongue, but she wouldn't let him take his time. She growled low in her throat and pressed her lips fiercely to his. He couldn't hold his control back any longer and met her, stroke for stroke. He'd never had anything that tasted as sweet as Anna Hollis did at that moment. The shy woman she'd been was gone, replaced with a fiery passion that burned him from the inside out.

"Touch me," she demanded.

He whirled her around, so her back was pressed against the desk, and he lifted her so she was barely sitting on the edge. The kiss was scorching, out of control, with a passion so intense he lost himself to the heat of it.

Things were moving faster than he'd anticipated, but he couldn't control his body, the instinct to mate prevalent in his mind. He bunched the red skirt around her waist so he could press his throbbing member to her wet heat.

"Oh God," she said, feeling him thrust against her, grinding slowly.

Only the barrier of his jeans and her red lace thong kept him from entering her. He could tell she was close to climaxing by the little whimpers she was making in the back of her throat.

Her pleasure would have to be enough for now. As much as he wanted to take her across the top of his desk, he knew a building full of people was not the place to do it. And besides, when he got her naked, he wanted her to stay that way for a long time. He knew he wouldn't be satisfied with having her only once.

Dylan leaned back to look at the woman in front of him, but kept their centers pressed close together. Their breaths were heaving, and he watched her shiver as he ran the tips of his fingers across her nipples, making them harden even more. Anna's eyes dilated at his touch and she inhaled quickly.

He took the zipper of her jacket between his fingers and brought it down slowly, inch by inch, until it sat open, showing hints of the red lace bra beneath it.

It was like opening a gift on Christmas morning—better than a gift. She was every fantasy come to life, and for the time being, she was all his. Her breasts were full and ripe, spilling from the cups of her bra with every breath. She was magnificent.

"Are you sure you want me to touch you?" he asked, skimming her nipples again with his knuckles.

She could barely speak, the sensations were so marvelous. "Yes," she said on a moan.

Dylan flipped the front clasp of her bra open and stared in wonder at the magnificent globes in front of him. He tweaked her nipples between his two fingers and squeezed gently, causing her to buck her pelvis against his own. He kissed her swollen mouth again, keeping up the duel assault on her nipples and clitoris.

"Do you like this?" he asked.

"Yes. . .yes. I want more."

"Tell me exactly what you want," he demanded.

"I want you inside me. I want you to fill me up," she panted. She was close to the edge, but he moved his fingers just shy of the sweet spot on her clitoris to prolong her pleasure. It was torture.

"How do you want me to fill you up?"

She was speechless. The effort it took to talk took too much out of her overly sensitized body.

"Do you want me to put my cock in your pussy?" he pushed relentlessly. "What about your mouth? Will you take it in your mouth and swallow everything I have to give you? How about your ass," he said, pushing his pinky down her drenched slit to the tiny puckered hole beneath.

"Oh, God. Yessssss," she screamed, and she bucked violently against his ministrations as she came in a violent crash of waves that took over her body and creamed his fingers. Sensations of light and color dimmed her vision until she thought she'd gone blind with the pleasure. She fell against him as exhaustion replaced passion.

"Oh my God," she said. "What was that?"

Dylan chuckled at her question, his need still raging in the lower half of his body. "That was an orgasm. The first of many you'll have with me."

"If I would have known it felt like this, I would have made some changes sooner," Anna said with a mischievous smile.

Dylan backed away from her slowly, his body a ticking time bomb, and winced at the discomfort of his straining erection.

"What about you?" she asked, noticing his pain.

"Today is not for me. It was an introduction of things to come, a demonstration of sorts. Not to mention the fact that I forgot to lock my office door, and we're taking a hell of a chance. But I'm not going to wait too much longer. I've wanted to fuck you for months."

He backed up quickly because he could tell that his words had reignited her arousal. He zipped up her jacket and helped her adjust her skirt. "Give me a few minutes to get my body under control, and we'll go meet with my architect before I change my mind and take you on the desk."

Anna looked like she wanted to take him up on the offer but got shakily to her feet and followed him to the door instead.

"I can't go out there like this," she said, referring to her slightly rumpled skirt and kiss swollen lips. "Do you think he'll know what we've been doing?"

"No," Dylan lied with a straight face.

Anyone would be able to tell what they'd been doing, especially Mitchell. He was no stranger to an aroused woman.

Anna looked like the morning after a wild night of passion. Her hair was tousled, her lipstick was gone and her face was flushed and dewy.

"I'll come by tonight as soon as I get off and we can finish what we've started. Does that sound like a good idea to you?" he asked, already counting down the minutes. He kissed her forehead gently and ushered her towards the door.

"Oh, yes," she answered. "We'll need to go somewhere else, because I wouldn't feel comfortable with you staying the night in the same house as my father. Even though we're in separate wings of the house, it's still too close for my comfort."

Dylan didn't bother to correct her assumption that he'd be spending the whole night with her. He never stayed the whole night. It was rule number one for staying unattached. He was going to strive to be the best teacher he could be. Of course, the benefits were more than rewarding if she was an apt pupil, and he had every reason to believe she would be after their first encounter.

Anna walked out to the parking lot in front of the offices of Maguire Homes with her legs still shaking. The sun beat down on her drained body, and the pavement felt unsteady beneath her feet. Earth-shattering was the only way she could think to describe her first encounter with Dylan Maguire.

The meeting with Mitchell had been embarrassing to say the least, her mind unable to stay focused on telling him exactly what she wanted for a house. All she could think about was the feel of Dylan's lips against hers.

She stopped at her car and dug her keys out of her bag. They always seemed to end up at the very bottom amidst all the other junk she carried around. She didn't notice the note until she'd gotten behind the wheel. The piece of yellow paper placed under her windshield wiper was like a flag flapping in the breeze.

"Uhh," she groaned, getting out of the car once again. All she wanted to do was go home, take a hot shower, get into bed and get some sleep so she was at her best when Dylan came to pick her up. Being a sex kitten was harder than she'd thought it would be. Her mind was already wandering, thinking of a relaxing evening at home when she opened the note.

*Dylan Maguire is mine. Stay away from him, slut. OR*

*ELSE.*

Anna stood on the pavement, her legs frozen at the words on the page. Dread roiled in her stomach along with something along the lines of disappointment. It didn't look like Dylan was going to be available to her after all. She'd have to think long and hard about whether or not he was worth the risk.

## CHAPTER FOUR

Dylan stood on the wide, covered front porch of the Hollis's plantation style house and rang the doorbell for the third time.

Under normal circumstances, his builder's curiosity would be amazed at the craftsmanship of a house over a hundred years old, one of the earliest built in Paradise. He'd run his hands along the large white columns that flanked the massive front doors of the Greek Revival Mansion, or inspect the hand cut glass that laid in the double-hung windows.

But not tonight. Tonight his mind was on one thing and one thing only. Well, two things. The first was obvious, which was the reason he was standing on Anna's front porch as anxious as a teenage boy on his first date. But the second…he was confused as to why no one was answering the door.

He sighed in relief as he saw lights flip on in various rooms of the house as the path was made to the front door. He looked down at his wristwatch to check the time. It wasn't that late, only eight-thirty, so he guessed Anna must have fallen asleep after their tête-à-tête earlier in the afternoon.

A satisfied smile flitted around his lips as he heard the deadbolts unlocked from the inside, but it disappeared when he saw it was Jack who answered the door instead of Anna.

"Hey Dylan, what brings you out here?"

Dylan found it a little awkward that Anna hadn't filled Jack in on their plans, but he knew it would take her some time to get used to their situation. Soon everyone in Paradise would know they were lovers. It was the way of a small town and he'd grown accustomed to the life.

"I'm supposed to pick Anna up. Is she ready to go?" He had an uneasy feeling in the pit of his stomach with the look Jack was giving him.

"She's not here," Jack said. "She left more than two hours ago. She just packed a bag and said she'd be gone for a couple of days, didn't even tell me where she was going." He stopped, scratched the stubble on his cheek and gave Dylan a considering glance. "What were you two meeting about this late for? Surely you can talk about the new house during office hours?"

"We weren't meeting about the house, Jack. I was picking her up for a date," Dylan said in his usual straightforward manner.

"Well it looks to me as if she decided not to go," Jack said.

"It's starting to look like that to me too. If she comes back will you tell her I stopped by?" Dylan said, already backing down the porch steps.

"Sure thing," Jack said as he closed the door.

Jack stood inside his empty house and wondered what the hell was going on. Anna had come home from her meeting with Dylan and immediately started packing her bags. He couldn't imagine what could have happened between there and home to make her stand up Dylan for a date, but he was going to find out.

He still believed they were perfect for each other. They just needed a little nudge in the right direction. Of course, his plans seemed to have backfired and they needed more than just a little nudge now. He couldn't imagine why two young people were so slow to pick up on the clues that stared them right in the face. They were obviously attracted to each other and they had common interests. What more could you need in a mate?

He'd had many happy years with Anna's mother, and

attraction and common interests were why they'd married.

And love, his subconscious reminded him. He'd loved that woman to distraction, and no other could ever take her place. He wanted Anna to experience that same feeling. He'd been so caught up in his own grief after his wife's death that he never stopped to think about the grief that a fifteen-year-old girl was experiencing. He'd let her fall into the role of caretaker, but that should have been his job.

Jack decided he was going to right as many wrongs as he could, but he just had to get her to cooperate.

Dylan pounded his fist against the steering wheel angrily and hung up his cell phone. Where was she? She was obviously avoiding him, wherever she was. What had happened to change her mind after she'd left his office? He knew in his gut that she was ready for what he had in store for her, but she was running scared.

His body was in excruciating pain. The pent up needs from earlier in the day had just accumulated over the hours until he was ready to burst.

It was probably a good thing he couldn't find her at this point. She wouldn't get the gentle introduction to lovemaking he had planned. He'd never been so angry or frustrated in his entire life.

He pulled out his cell phone again and started dialing Mitchell's phone number. He was surprised the tiny device wasn't crushed in his hand with as much force as he was using.

"Hello," Mitchell answered.

"Where are you?" Dylan said, without greeting.

"Nice to talk to you too, old buddy. I'm at Shiney's Pub. I take it by the growl in your voice that your plans didn't go as you thought they would."

"You could say that," Dylan said, his anger dissipating into depression. If he was smart he'd forget Anna and go find the satisfaction that his body needed. It wouldn't be difficult to find a warm bed and a willing woman, and he'd also be able to show Anna just what she threw away.

"Come on down and I'll buy you a beer and beat your ass at pool," Mitchell said. "It's not like you've got anything better to do. Besides, there are some fine looking women sitting around here all alone."

"I'll see you in a minute," Dylan said, disconnecting the phone.

Anna threw back another shot of tequila like it was tap water and continued to pace back and forth—with only the occasional stumble—across Mel's living room floor. She'd fled to her friend's house like a coward after being warned to stay away from Dylan.

"I can't believe you stood up Dylan Maguire," Mel said for the thousandth time. "I don't think anyone has ever done that before. You'll be a legend in Paradise: *The one woman who said, No.* I can see the headlines in the *Paradise Today* now."

"Thanks, Mel. You're really making me feel better," Anna said.

After finding the note on the windshield of her car, she'd decided to ignore it and keep her plans with Dylan for evening. After all, it would be hard to turn Dylan down if he was going to give her an experience like she'd had in his office. She'd have to be an idiot.

She'd changed her mind when the black sedan behind her tried to run her off the road. The note was a childish prank. Being run off a bridge going fifty miles an hour to crash and burn on the jagged rocks beneath was serious business. Someone was determined to keep Dylan Maguire for their own. And she wasn't one to ignore clues that stared her in the face. Apparently someone else didn't want to give up the mind shattering orgasms he'd bestowed as well.

"I'm just saying," Mel continued, "There are plenty of women in this town who'd be happy to share Dylan Maguire's bed for one night. But now that I think about it, you and I might be the only two women in Paradise he hasn't slept with. The man's a legend."

"That's comforting. At least I could have learned from an expert," Anna said. "And that means the note could be from anyone." She poured another shot of tequila and drank it down, each one getting easier and easier.

"Maybe you should slow down on the alcohol, Anna. You've never been much of a drinker."

Mel looked at the half-empty bottle of Tequila that sat on the coffee table and shuddered. She hadn't drunk anything because she had to open the bookstore the following morning. That meant Anna had finished that much of the bottle all by herself.

"And why not? I'm tired of being the sensible good girl. I want to be the woman in town that fills all the beauty parlors with gossip for the next six months. I want to be dangerous and daring, and if I want to sleep with Dylan Maguire, why should I let some maniac in a black Oldsmobile stop me?"

"I can't imagine," Mel said, shaking her head.

"Is there anyone that you can think of who could do something like this?" Anna asked, forming a plan in her mind. She'd draw the culprit out, and they'd have a showdown the whole town would talk about for the next twenty years. She wasn't letting Dylan go without a fight. Her need for sexual fulfillment was just as great as anyone's. It would be just like the movies.

"He dated Veronica Fox for almost a year," Mel said, chewing on her bottom lip. "That's an eternity for a man like Dylan. He's definitely love-'em-and-leave-'em material."

"The same Veronica Fox we went to school with?" Anna asked with a gulp. "The same Veronica Fox that was homecoming queen and head cheerleader?"

"The one and only," Mel said. "But she doesn't seem like the type to kill you behind your back. She seems more up front to me. She'd probably try to hit you head on so her face was the last thing you saw. Either that, or just shoot you at point blank range. But I don't think she's an option. I like Veronica. She's always been very nice to me."

"Yeah, me too, but people change," Anna said. "I can't believe I didn't know they'd dated. I'll put her on my list of suspects. How long could it possibly be in a town this small?"

"That's because you've lived with your head buried in the sand for the last ten years. She and Dylan were real hot and heavy for a while, but word is that he called it off because she was pressuring him about marriage.

"Who'd you hear that from?" Anna asked.

"Who else? My mother." Mel said. If anybody knew anything in Paradise, it was Margaret James. "She got it straight from Veronica's mother who said she'd already picked out her dress and rented the church when he called it quits. She was apparently devastated."

"Huh," Anna said, weaving towards the couch. "I can't imagine buying a dress and renting the church before he even proposed. I would have ordered the cake first because you can always eat that. All you can do with a dress is watch it turn yellow, and then you get depressed because you realize you're nearing thirty and you're still not married."

"Wow, thanks for that visual," Mel said, wishing she'd had at least one shot. "I only have five years before I'm thirty."

All this thinking made Anna's brain hurt, and the sloshing in her belly wasn't making her feel so hot either. "I can't believe he'd break it off with someone that looks like Veronica. I'd even go out with Veronica if I was into women. I just love her hair. Maybe I should dye mine black. How do you think I'd look?"

"Like Elvira," Mel said. "Stick with your natural color. Dylan is attracted to you now, remember?"

"Yeah, but I stood him up. Do you think I blew my chances?"

"Knowing his reputation, probably. But you might still have a chance if you want to go for it," Mel said. "It's not like you have anything to lose."

"I'll have to do it tomorrow. I don't think I'm at my best right now. I'll explain the whole situation. Surely he'll understand once he knows the circumstances." Anna stood up slowly and put her hands on her head to stop the spinning. "I think I'm going to be sick," she said on her way to the bathroom.

"Well that'll impress him," Mel said to Anna's retreating back.

Shiney's Pub had been a fixture in Paradise for almost a hundred years. It had seen most of its patrons go off to war and witnessed prohibition, but its doors were still open. Four generations that carried the Shiney name had worked behind the long expanse of mahogany bar that had held many a drink. Despite its tavern atmosphere, they held family night every Thursday, just like they had since their doors first opened.

Dylan opened the glass-paned front door and searched for Mitchell in the smoky interior. The place was only half full on a Monday night, but there was still a respectable crowd.

It was a place that people came to after work to unwind or a place to party on the weekends. Circular tables were scattered on the wide planked pine floor, but the bar was the centerpiece where high-backed stools lined their way down the worn mahogany. A large mirror ran down the wall on the backside of the bar, and dozens of bottles stood in front of it, their reflections multiplied.

Dylan waved to a few individuals he knew and headed towards the bar. Brian Shiney IV was behind the counter pouring whatever was on tap into mugs and talking to Douglas Howard, the owner of Howard's Grocery.

"Hey, Brian," Dylan said. "Mr. Howard," he nodded to the ancient man sitting on the stool.

"What's going on, Dylan?" Brian said. "Can I pour you a drink?"

"Make it two, and I'll take one back to Mitchell," Dylan said, putting his money on the bar. "You look pretty busy for a Monday night."

"Yeah, we're doing okay. The nights are getting warmer, and people are starting to get out more. There's only so much you can do closed up in a house all winter," Brian said with a wink.

*Yeah, I know*, Dylan thought with a sigh. He was supposed to be doing it right now. He grabbed both mugs and headed back to the room that housed the pool tables.

Mitchell was playing pool in the center of the room while a table of women were attempting to play their own game, but they couldn't keep their eyes off of his backside long enough to make a decent shot.

Dylan shook his head in amusement. It was the same

everywhere they went. Women were attracted to Mitchell like bees were to honey, not to say that he didn't score his own fair share of looks either. Fortunately, he and Mitchell both happened to be lovers of all women, and they all loved them right back.

"That was a lousy shot," Dylan said, setting his beer down and picking up a cue stick. "I'll beat you in no time if you're gonna play that bad."

"In your dreams buddy. I'm willing to bet that your mind is going to be so preoccupied with what you could be doing at this very moment, that you won't make a shot." Mitchell stood, propped against his cue stick, with a competitive grin on his face.

Dylan scowled at his friend's accurate statement and got ready to break. Unfortunately, Mitchell couldn't have been more right as to where his mind was, not a single ball went in the pockets.

"Shit," Dylan said. "What the hell could make her change her mind and run like that?" he asked.

"I don't know my friend. Maybe you came on a little strong. I mean, the woman comes to our office to get a new house and you give her an orgasm on your desk. Maybe it was more than she bargained for."

Dylan shot Mitchell a dirty look. "How the hell do you know what happened on my desk?"

"My office is right next to yours, and we have really thin walls. I'm pretty sure the whole building heard what the two of you were doing. Anna is definitely a moaner. Janet was talking to a new client, and I thought she was going to have a heart attack with all that noise going on."

Dylan threw the chalk at Mitchell's head, which he easily ducked. "I should just move on and chalk Anna up as a loss, but I want her so damn bad."

"Well, my friend," Mitchell said, looking towards the door, "The opportunity to move forward has just arrived. A blast from your past just walked through the door, and she looks like she'd be willing to take Anna's place for the night."

Dylan looked over his shoulder and gave a mental groan. He did not need this tonight of all nights. The woman grabbed her beer and kept her eyes intense on his. She was a magnificent specimen of womanhood.

"Hey, Veronica," Dylan said. "What brings you to Shiney's?" His already primed body leapt painfully at the woman in front of him, and his breath caught deep in his chest, making his heart throb in time with the bass from the stereo. Sex had never been a weakness between the two of them when they were involved, and his dick had chosen that moment to reminisce about old times.

"I just closed up the store and decided to unwind with a drink," Veronica said, standing close enough that their bodies touched.

She owned a little boutique called *Veronica's Closet* that sold women's clothing and lingerie. It was located on the other side of the square and was indeed a short walk to Shiney's.

Dylan willed his body under control and took a small step back. She looked as hot as ever, her thick black hair trailing down her back and her light blue eyes made up like a gypsy's. The long skirt and stretchy top she wore were the exact shade as her eyes, and they fit her body like a glove. She was one sexy lady, but the image of another sexy lady in the throws of her first climax intruded his thoughts. There would be no other women until he'd had Anna, no matter how frustrated he was, which made him even more furious at her for her desertion.

"Can I buy you a drink, stranger?" she asked, closing the distance he tried to put between them.

Veronica was close enough that he could smell the scent she wore, and the look in her eyes was an invitation in itself. She intoxicated him, and she clouded his judgment. It would be so easy to press his body closer to hers and take what he so desperately needed. But it would be wrong to substitute one woman for another. He wouldn't do that to Anna, assuming he still had a chance with her. And he wouldn't do it to Veronica. He still cared about her a great deal, just not enough to marry her.

"I was actually just getting ready to leave," Dylan

said, handing her his cue stick and backing away. "I've got an early appointment in the morning, and I need to get home and get some sleep. Mitchell's probably game for a free drink though."

"What do you say, Mitchell, are you up for a free drink?" Veronica asked, undaunted by Dylan's rejection.

"Absolutely, babe, and I'll kick your ass instead of Dylan's," he said giving Dylan the sign that he had everything under control. "A man does need a challenge every once in a while."

"I hope you won't be making shots like I saw earlier," Veronica said. "You'll need some pretty wide pockets."

Dylan winced on his way out the door as he heard her comment, knowing she'd caught him in a lie about him needing to leave. She'd probably walked in right after he had. It was just as well though. His time with Veronica was long over, and he was going to be up bright and early banging on Anna's front door until she answered. He deserved an explanation after the restless night he was about to spend alone.

## CHAPTER FIVE

Anna rolled out of bed at six thirty the next morning, her mind alert and ready to face the day. She pulled on a pair of sweats and shuffled into the kitchen, not looking quite as good as she felt.

Her hair was pulled up in a haphazard ponytail, and she smelled like the inside of a bottle of Tequila. Fortunately, she had time to make repairs.

Mel was already up and dressed and pouring a generous amount of cream into her coffee. One side of her hair was flattened from sleep. And she stifled a yawn when she noticed Anna enter the room.

"I can't believe you're up this early," Mel said, surprised and a little jealous. She'd never been much of a morning person.

"I feel great," Anna said. "I'm energized and ready to

explain things to Dylan. If he'll listen. And hopefully you'll be looking at a new woman tomorrow."

"That is so wrong," Mel complained. "You're beautiful, you're about to have great sex and you don't get hangovers. Life is so unfair."

Anna laughed and gathered up all her things. "I'm going to go ahead and take off. I need to shower and spruce up a little before I corner down Dylan at his office. I don't even have the man's cell number."

"Just make sure you keep me up to date on what happens. Not everyone leads a life as exciting as yours," Mel said, waving Anna out the door.

Anna jogged to her car, her steps light, humming a Celine Dion song from a car commercial she'd heard. It was a beautiful March morning. Spring was in the air and everything was going her way. She quashed down the little niggling of doubt she had at telling Dylan the truth when she saw another note on her windshield.
"You big bully," she muttered to no one in particular. She took the note from under her wiper blades and tore it into little pieces without reading it. She watched the little pieces fall to the ground and she quashed the guilt she felt for littering in Mel's front yard. Sometimes life called for a little dramatics.

"This is ridiculous," she shouted to the neighborhood in general. "We're adults. If you have a problem, stop being a coward and meet me face to face."

Anna crossed her fingers and hoped that no one would respond. She hopped in her car without glancing around to see if anyone actually took her up on her offer, and backed down Mel's driveway. She looked uneasily at the wooded park across the street, imagining dozens of eyes tracking her every move.

She made it home in record time and hurried in the house, thankful that her father had already left for the store. She didn't have time to answer any of the questions he was sure to have. She was on a mission to grovel and seduce. Nothing was going to stop her.

She piled her hair up high on her head and jumped in the shower. Anna had already decided she was going to do everything she could possibly think of to convince Dylan to take the day off. It was time to pull out the big guns. She'd corner him in his office and not give him a chance to say anything but yes. Of course, she'd need to lure him to a place outside of his office, a place that offered them a little privacy. She wasn't sure she could take any more strange looks like the last time she was there.

Anna put her hand to her stomach to quiet the butterflies dancing around. It was hard to remember she was no longer a shy wallflower. Hopefully, being an outgoing sex kitten wouldn't lead to ulcers.

She rubbed lotion on her entire body and selected the sexiest lingerie she owned out of her drawer. A purchase she'd recently bought on her life changing shopping trip.

"Thank you, Mel," she said quietly, touching the soft lace between her fingers. It was a simple black teddy, but the sheer lace didn't leave anything for the imagination. "Eat your heart out, Dylan Maguire."

She pulled on a sleek black jump-suit that zipped up the front and released her hair from its clip so it curled down her back.

"Okay," she said looking at herself in the mirror, "That's as good as it's going to get."

Anna made her way to the kitchen and popped a couple of slices of bread in the toaster. She hadn't had anything to eat since lunch the day before. No wonder the tequila had had such an effect on her.

She looked at her reflection in the side of the toaster and cleared her throat, practicing her apologetic, but seductive, expression she'd need to use on Dylan.

"Dylan," she started, batting her eyelashes a little. "I just wanted to apologize for running away from you yesterday. You see, one of your crazy ex-girlfriends has been threatening me, and I wasn't sure that one orgasm was worth dying for."

The toaster popped out her bread and she jumped back a little, surprised. She'd really gotten into her speech.

"I can't say that," she groaned, rolling her eyes. "No one would believe that story. I'll have to show him the notes."

She thought for a minute while buttering her toast. Maybe she should just take the more direct approach. She looked at her reflection in the toaster again, pouted her lips out Angelina Jolie style and stuck out her chest.

"Take me Dylan. I'm yours," she said, licking her lips provocatively.

The doorbell interrupted her rehearsal, and she started laughing at her ridiculousness on the way to the door. She had plenty of time to think of something. She would just be herself and let things happen how they were supposed to happen.

Anna looked at the Grandfather clock that sat in the foyer of the Hollis Mansion, its pendulum swinging slowly in a hypnotic rhythm. It was barely eight o'clock in the morning.

"Who could this be? I don't have time for any setbacks," she mumbled, jerking the door open with more force than necessary.

Her mouth froze in an open "O" when she saw a very annoyed Dylan standing on the other side of the threshold. Her mouth opened and closed several times with no words coming out, so she resembled a surprised fish.

"I see my presence makes you speechless," Dylan said, walking through the open door.

"I...I just wasn't expecting you this early," Anna said, mentally cursing herself for stuttering and backing away. She looked weak, nothing like the sex kitten she'd been practicing.

"I was just on my way to see you so I could explain." Anna backed into the formal dining room and went behind the couch, hoping the object would be enough of a separation to keep him at bay for the moment. "It really is a good explanation."

"I'm not really in the mood for any of your explanations," Dylan said.

He followed her around the couch and they circled each other slowly, like two boxers in the ring. "You have one chance to answer me honestly," he said. "Do you still want me?"

Anna stood frozen, unable to believe her ears. She still had a chance after all. She would explain everything afterwards, but right now she had a lot of pent up frustration she needed to release, and by the feral look in Dylan's eyes he was suffering the same fate.

"Yes," she said, her voice hoarse and her body

trembling.

Dylan jumped over the couch, eliminating any protection she thought she had. Her adrenaline was pounding and she instinctively started to run away from him, like the prey she felt she was.

Anna heard him growl seconds before she felt his grip on her arm. She yelped in surprise at the sting of his fingers, and gasped as he spun her around to face him. He backed her against the wall and closed his hand around her throat, pressing his thumb on her throbbing pulse.

Her turquoise eyes were wide and her chest was heaving in anticipation and a little fear. She watched as he brought his other hand up and slowly pulled on the zipper of her jumpsuit, teasing her exposed flesh with raspy fingers.

Dylan held his breath as he saw the filmy lace that was being revealed. He'd been painfully hard all night, but the sight of her pale flesh took him beyond any need he'd ever experienced.

Anna reevaluated her situation. Was this the way she wanted to come to Dylan? As a pliant partner that he could direct at his command? She wasn't giving him the challenge that his personality seemed to call for. She was just submitting without giving as good as she got.

She brought her hand up and enclosed Dylan's wrist,

making him raise his eyebrow at her bold attempt to stop him. She brought her other hand up and placed her palm on his chest, tracing his toned muscles with her fingernails and making him draw in a sharp breath at her touch.

Anna inhaled deeply, the yearning and desire too intense for her primed body. She had to get herself under control. She steadied her resolve and pushed with all her might. She watched Dylan fall backward, but didn't stop to see the look on his face. She took off at a dead run and erupted into a fit of giggles.

The chase was on.

She took off up the wide staircase that led to the top two floors at full speed, but curiosity got the better of her and she turned to see Dylan close on her heels headed in the same direction, a competitive smile dancing on his lips.

Her distraction was her downfall because her foot got caught on the carpet runner and she went down on one knee. She flung her hands out to catch her fall and winced and the carpet burns that reddened her palms. That was all the advantage Dylan needed to catch her.

"So you want to play, do you?" Dylan said, hardly breathing heavy at all after a run up a flight of stairs. He pushed her against the wall of the second floor landing and took her mouth in a savage kiss.

Anna groaned at the feel of his lips against hers, the

pain in her hands forgotten. It was even better than she remembered, the feel of his hard body against hers as he devoured her mouth with his kiss. She wrapped her legs around his waist and tore at the buttons of his shirt, desperate to feel his flesh against hers. He stripped her so the only thing she wore was the swatch of black lace.

"Holy mother of God," Dylan panted. His gaze scorched her already enflamed body. "Please tell me you have more of these."

Her hands went to the snap of his jeans and worked frantically to reach her goal. She slipped her hands into his waistband and found their target, inciting a groan from Dylan. "I have a whole drawer full. I bought them thinking of you."

He was heavy in her hand, thick and pulsing with the same desire she felt. She kissed her way down his torso, reveling in the different textures she found on her journey—the rigid muscles and planes of his chest and stomach, the light smattering of hair that tickled her lips.

She nipped with teeth and tongue at the muscular indention at his waist and then again on the inside of his thigh, bypassing the object of her desire with teasing grazes of her hair and cheek. Dylan threaded his fingers through her hair and brought her closer and she inhaled the muskiness of his scent. Moisture pooled between her thighs and she looked up at his through lowered lids. His head was thrown back in surrender, his muscles taut with anticipation.

She touched her tongue to the lone bead of liquid that had gathered at the tip of his cock, and he jumped in response. He was hard and heavy, veins rigid and the mushroom head of his cock swollen. His sac was full and tight, and she cupped it gently I her hand while taking his shaft in the other. She could barely get her fingers around him.

Anna took her time savoring the taste of him, running her tongue from the base of his cock to the tip before taking him completely in her mouth.

"God, Anna," he groaned. "You're killing me."

She moaned around him and felt him jerk in her mouth from the vibrations. His grip on her hair grew tighter. She relaxed her throat and swallowed him down as far as she could, working the flat of her tongue against the sensitive underside of his cock.

"Stop, I'm going to come," he gasped out, pulling her away from him.

"Mmm, I hope so." She tongued his sac while he raged a silent war as if to let her continue.

"I want to be inside you when I come."

"We have all day. And night," she purred. "Come in my mouth. I want to taste you."

Dylan couldn't resist her plea, and she smiled in triumph. She took him back in her mouth, bobbing her head quickly now up and down his cock. She sucked him down and felt him stiffen above her before the first spurt of come shot down her throat. His moans were like music to her ears, and his seed tasted like nothing she'd ever experienced. It was its own aphrodisiac and she knew she could become addicted.

Dylan collapsed to his knees in front of her, grabbing her in an embrace. Her own lust was spiraling out of control. Her juices ran down her thighs, and she pressed her mound against the rough fabric of his jeans trying to sate her own passion. Anna's ears rang with lust, and it got louder until she thought she'd pass out with the intensity.

"Anna," Dylan said, gritting his teeth and holding her tight to him. "My phone's ringing."

"What?" Anna asked, still unsure of what he was saying. She rubbed against him again and stifled her moan in his chest. She was almost there. She'd never needed to come so bad in her life.

"I said my phone's ringing," he repeated.

"Who cares," she said frustrated. "I'm this close to coming, and you're going to stop because your phone's ringing?" Hysteria tinged her voice.

"It's my private line," he explained, trying to pull his

pants up so he could dig at the phone in his pocket. "Mitchell wouldn't call me unless it was an emergency. I swear I'll make it up to you. I'll give you so many orgasms you'll pass out from the pleasure."

"You'd damn well better. I'm feeling rather violent at the moment." The phone stopped ringing and Anna stood up and leaned against the stair railing, her legs unsteadier than she thought they'd be. She stripped out of the damp teddy and took satisfaction as Dylan's eyes glazed over with lust. She gave him a wink and bounded up the stairs to her room.

He pulled off his jeans, his cock already springing to life, and followed her. The phone started ringing again just as he reached her bedroom door.

"Shit," he said, fumbling for the phone.

Anna laughed hysterically at the sight of Dylan. He wore nothing but his socks and was fumbling with his jeans to get them turned right side out before digging through the pockets.

"What?" Dylan yelled into the receiver. "This had better be a life or death situation, Mitchell, because if it's not I swear to God…"

Anna smiled as his words trailed off. She'd crawled up on the bed and sat on her knees so her moist pussy was bared to him. She cupped her breasts in her hands, tweaking the nipples until they hardened into stiff peaks.

She let her hand drop and roamed down her belly until it came to the small strip of dark curls at the juncture of her thighs. She dipped a finger into the syrup that covered her mound and moaned.

Dylan snapped the phone shut and dropped it on the floor, never hearing a word of what Mitchell had to say. He started toward her like a predator on the hunt, but he'd barely moved before the phone started ringing again.

Dylan sighed and ran his fingers through his hair, visibly counting to ten before he reached down to grab the phone.

"Dammit, Mitchell, what do you want?" Dylan asked, his voice hoarse with desire and frustration.

"Sorry to interrupt, but you need to come down to the Willis site," Mitchell said.

"I'm not coming down there just so Mrs. Willis can tell me how much she loves what I've done with the house, but could I please just change her walk-in closet one more time to accommodate another pair of shoes she's bought." Dylan pressed his fingers against his eyes. "Now if that's all…"

"The house is on fire," Mitchell interrupted.

"What did you say?"

"I said the house is on fire and arson is suspected.

The fire chief wants you down here ten minutes ago so he can ask you some questions."

Dylan hung up without saying good bye and started pulling his clothes back on in earnest. "I've got to get to one of my sites. Someone just burned a million dollar home to the ground."

He looked around for his shirt and didn't see it anywhere. "Where the hell's my shirt?"

Anna pulled on the pair of jeans she'd bought like Mel's and a tight green t-shirt, before leading Dylan back into the hallway. She started giggling as soon as she saw his shirt dangling from the chandelier over the stairs. He rolled his eyes at her and jumped up to grab it.

"I think I need to go with you," Anna said over peels of laughter. She slipped on flip-flops and pulled her hair back into a loose tail. There was nothing she could do about her kiss swollen lips or the beard burn on her neck, but the rest of her looked pretty presentable.

"This will be no place for you. It's bound to be crowded, and it could be very messy when there's this much money involved." He headed towards the front door with Anna hot on his heels. "Are you ready to let the whole town know that we want to jump each other's bones?"

*Oh, low blow.* "This has to do with why I ran away from you last night," Anna said, ignoring his question.

"It's forgotten, Anna, as long as you still want me I can forgive a case of nerves."

"It's not nerves," Anna said, stubbornly. "I think someone is trying to kill me."

## CHAPTER SIX

"What?" Dylan asked, stopping dead in his tracks.

"Are you going to let me come with you or not?"

"Get in the truck, and tell me what the hell is going on."

Anna followed behind him and got in the beat up Ford truck that Dylan drove for work everyday. His image didn't seem to fit the battered automobile, but there were obviously quirks he harbored she didn't know about. Like his recent penchant for bossing her around. She'd have to break him of that habit.

Dylan revved the truck and took off down the long paved driveway in front of the Hollis Mansion. "Now start talking," Dylan ordered.

"You know, there's no reason for you to talk to me

that way. I'm the one being threatened. You could at least be a little sympathetic. And polite," she added as an afterthought.

Dylan rolled his eyes and took a right over the bridge that headed towards the outskirts of town where the Willis' had chosen to build their dream home. The middle-aged couple was wealthy and had nothing better to do with their time than be a pain in his ass, but they were good customers.

"I apologize," Dylan said sarcastically. "Please tell me why you think someone is trying to kill you."

Anna nodded her head at him primly, princess to peasant. He almost laughed when he thought of how shy he thought she'd been when first seeing her. She'd obviously only been out of practice.

"Well, after that first day we met in your office," Anna began, blushing furiously and thinking about what they'd been doing ten minutes after being formally introduced, "I found a note on my windshield that told me to stay away from you."

Dylan interrupted her. "That's why you ran from me? Because some jealous woman told you to? I thought you'd have more spine than that."

"Excuse me, Mr. I won't let you finish a damn sentence," Anna shot back, giving as good as she got. She was getting tired of high and mighty Dylan Maguire. She might have been shy for the last ten years, but that didn't mean she was a doormat. "If you'll be so kind as to shut up I'll finish."

Dylan mumbled something inaudible under his breath, which Anna took as a sign to keep talking. "As I was saying, I received the note right after I left your office, but I just chalked it up to a childish prank by one of your ex-girlfriends. I had fully planned to ignore it and meet you anyway," Anna said, giving him a pointed look.

Dylan did have the sense to look a little abashed at her confession. "It was on the way home that I ran into trouble. A black car tailed me through town and across Paradise Crossing."

Paradise Crossing was a beam bridge that allowed cars to travel over Hollis Creek and enter the town. There was one way in and one way out of Paradise. "I noticed the car coming up beside me and thought he was just trying to pass, but he was trying to edge me to the side. I swerved to avoid him and barely missed scraping the side of my car against the railing."

Dylan let out a slow, controlled breath at Anna's story. The two incidences happening so close together were probably more than just coincidence. "You said *He*," Dylan said.

"What?" Anna said confused.

"When you mentioned the driver of the car you said

he," Dylan repeated. "Did you actually see a man behind the wheel of the car?"

"No, now that you mention it, I didn't. I was just using a generalization," Anna said. "The windows were a really dark tint, and I couldn't see through them. To tell you the truth, the only thing I was really paying attention to was staying on the road."

"Shit," Dylan said as the visual of what could have happened to Anna went through his mind. "I'll check into this, Anna. I'm not on bad terms with anyone I've dated in the past. I can't think of one single person that would do something like that."

Anna stewed a little. She really wanted to keep up the hope that Veronica Fox was the culprit. The woman was just too perfect. Surely she had some schizophrenic tendencies to take away the flawless edge.

"And I can't imagine that your incidences and the fire at the Willis place are related," Dylan said. "More than likely it was a couple of punk kids looking for something to destroy."

Dylan slowly pulled the truck onto the graveled lane that led to the house and watched the pandemonium taking place around him. The house was a total loss. He could tell just by looking. They'd have to bulldoze away the remains and start from scratch. It looked like he was going to be spending another ten months with the Willis's.

He could see Mitchell talking to Chief Russ Davies, a look of irritation on his face.

"Looks like this is going to be fun," Dylan said. "I don't suppose I can convince you to stay in the truck."

"No, but I appreciate you making the concession so graciously," Anna said, patting his hand and opening the truck door.

The ground was muddy with soot and debris, and she had to watch her step to avoid nails or other sharp objects from piercing the soles of her shoes. She followed closely on Dylan's heels as he headed in Mitchell's direction.

Mitchell looked weary in her opinion. His eyes were drawn and worried and the tie he usually wore knotted crisply at his throat was shoved in his front pocket, but he still put on his charmer's smile for her benefit and kissed her hand.

"Good to see you again, Anna," he said. "No wonder Dylan didn't want to be interrupted." He gave her a wink and turned his attention to Dylan.

"What's going on Mitchell?" Dylan asked. "Have they found the cause of the fire?"

"Yeah," he said. "It's nothing too complicated. Gasoline and matches. It works the same way every time. With all the raw insulation lying around, the place went up like a tinder box."

Anna was watching Chief Davies out of the corner of her eye. The man was collecting every scrap of information he could find and you could practically see the wheels turning in his head. She'd known him since birth and always thought he looked like a comfortable sort of man, if not overly bright or terribly thorough.

His family was considered new to the area—since he and his wife had moved to Paradise some forty years before when they were still newlyweds—instead of being third or fourth generation like a good majority of the town's residents.

She couldn't imagine him rummaging around in the ashes looking for clues to the fire. It would take far more effort than he was willing to expend. He was the kind of man that ate jelly donuts behind his desk while his feet were propped up on a growing stack of files. No, she didn't think this case was one that was likely to be solved.

Chief Davies cleared his throat and got both men's attention. "I need to ask you some questions for the investigation, Dylan," he began, wiping the sweat off his brow with the red handkerchief he always left hanging out of his back pocket.

"Can you think of anyone that would do something like this?" Chief Davies asked. "Someone who maybe has a grudge against you? Previous employers, old friends, old lovers?" The chief looked apologetically at Anna about mentioning the word lovers in a ladies presence.

"No," Dylan said. "I haven't had any problems with past clients or friends. There's no one that I can think of that would do something this juvenile."

"I understand that you've been working on this house for almost a year?" the chief continued. "Isn't that a little long for building a house?"

"My clients are just a little harder to please than most," Dylan said, smiling grimly at the thought of the Willis's. It was not going to be fun starting this project over with them. "They find something new they like almost every day and want us to add it or rip out what we've already done and start anew. That's the only reason it's taken so long. We would have been finished with it in the next six weeks if this hadn't have happened."

"I understand that this house was pretty heavily insured," Davies said, waiting patiently for Dylan's reaction.

"All of my houses are insured while we're working on them," Dylan said. "It's how we keep from losing our shirts if something like this happens."

"It just seems coincidental to me that a couple that caused you as many headaches as the Willis's did end up having their house burned to the ground."

"Chief Davies," Dylan said, shortly. "This home cost us a little over a million dollars to build. If it costs us that much to build you can imagine the retail value of the home. It is definitely in my best interest to see it finished. We get a large percentage of the total cost. I would not cut my own throat financially speaking by burning down my next paycheck. I have been described as a lot of things but never stupid."

Anna gasped at his words. It had finally dawned on her what the chief had been insinuating. Dylan could have no more done something like that than she could have.

"Chief Davies," Anna said, her voice scolding. "You should be ashamed of yourself for even thinking for one minute that Dylan had anything to do with something of this nature."

"Now Anna," the chief stuttered. "I have to check out all the avenues to get this investigation solved. In most cases, the easiest answer is usually the right answer."

"Well it's not the right answer this time," she said. "Dylan has been with me all morning, so it is impossible that he did what you're suggesting. Martha would be as disappointed as I am to know that you think someone like Dylan could be responsible for this."

Martha Davies was not a woman you wanted to mess with. Formidable was the first word that came to Anna's mind when she thought of her. She could put the fear of God into every man, woman and child in Paradise at just the mention of her name, and Anna took a little satisfaction to see the pallor of the chief's face pale considerably at the mention of his wife.

"I'm sure it's all a big misunderstanding," the chief hurried to assure her. "I'm just trying to be thorough and do my job. The citizens of Paradise are my first concern, but I'm sure Dylan had nothing to do with this mess."

He was sweating profusely at the thought of the skinning he'd get if his wife ever found out that he'd upset Anna Hollis.

The Hollis's were practically royalty in the town, and his wife was determined to run in the same circles. Hollis Tools had single handedly kept the town afloat during the Depression, and small towns had long memories. He didn't want to give them the chance to be angry at him for the unforeseeable future.

Dylan had to cover his mouth and look down at his shoes to keep from laughing at the cornered expression on the chief's face. Anna was giving the man hell, and if he didn't step in soon things were liable to get ugly. Mitchell made no effort to cover up his smile and grinned from ear to ear.

"It's all right, Anna." Dylan said, taking her by the arm. "The more information the chief has the sooner he can find out who did all this."

"That is still no reason to treat a prosperous, tax paying citizen like a common criminal," Anna said.

"You're right, Anna," the chief jumped in, trying to make good on his earlier blunder. "I apologize for the insinuation. More than likely it was just a couple of kids fooling around looking for trouble." Anna looked mildly appeased at his apology and decided the matter was settled.

"Dylan, you'll need to meet with the insurance agents and file a report. Looks like you're going to have to start over. I know the Willis's, and I don't envy you having to break the news to them."

The truth was, in a town the size of Paradise, the Willis's had probably had a dozen phone calls already. Everybody knew everybody else's business in the small town, and secrets were hard to come by.

Dylan shook Chief Davies' hand graciously, and they all watched, huddled in a tight circle, as the chief hefted himself into his two-ton pickup truck.

"Anna, it is always a pleasure," Mitchell said, giving her an affectionate slap on the back. "And always entertaining. I'm out of here you two. I've got to get back to the office and get to work on your house," he said to Anna. "I take it you won't be in today?" he asked Dylan.

"It's okay," Anna interrupted, turning to Dylan. "I know you've got a lot of things to take care of. We can meet later on if you like. I can get someone to swing me by the house on their way through town."

Anna looked around at the dozens of officers and firemen that were milling around the scene. The crime rate was low in Paradise, so when something of this nature occurred they all felt they should make an appearance and take part in the investigation.

"You have no idea how badly I want to go back to your place and finish what we started." He moved in close so he held her in a loose embrace. "Even now all I can think about is being inside you."

Anna shivered at his words. "Don't think I've forgotten that things were very one sided before." She leaned up and nipped at his ear, uncaring of the curious stares and whispers of the city officials around them. "You've left me in a very tenuous position. All it would take is a small touch to make me come. Maybe I should just go home and finish what you started by myself."

Dylan growled. "Don't you dare. In fact, I forbid you from touching yourself until I can watch you."

"And what's the punishment if I disobey?"

"Torture. I'll see how many hours I can bring you right to the edge without giving you release. You'll be begging me before it's over. Promise me you won't touch yourself. I'll know if you do."

"I promise," Anna said shakily.

"Good. Why don't we meet at Shiney's tonight? Where something sexy. I'll teach you how to play pool. And then…we'll finish what we started."

"Why can't we just get right to it? Are you determined to torture me no matter what?"

"I'm afraid if I don't give myself enough time to cool down, then I'll just take you wherever we're standing. If there are people around I can at least get control of myself. I don't want to hurt you. Or scare you."

"You could never hurt me, Dylan," she said, touching his cheek. "I'm stronger than you think. And I'm willing to be a little adventurous with you. Only you."

"I'm going to hold you to that."

Anna gave him a quick kiss and moved away to catch a ride with one of the deputies leaving the scene. "Try to take it easy on me at pool. It's my first time."

# CHAPTER SEVEN

"Are you sure you don't mind coming with me?" Anna asked Mel as she checked her appearance in the mirror of her bedroom. She was more nervous now than she was the first time she stepped foot in Dylan's office. Her body was primed, and any touch against her sensitive skin was its own kind of torture. The last place she wanted to be was in a room full of curious eyes. But she'd play Dylan's game. And by the time she was finished with him he'd be begging.

"Of course I don't mind," Mel said, stifling a yawn. "I'm always happy to watch you trounce some poor sucker at pool. I just hope Dylan's a good loser."

Anna watched Mel lounge back across her bed, her feet crossed and a magazine spread open on her lap, with envy. She wished she could have some of the natural spark that Mel exuded. She was just a fun and bubbly person, and you could tell by looking. Her dark hair was tousled and her ripped jeans showed off her curvy body. She wore another t-shirt that exposed the gold dangles in her belly button. No one but Anna knew that Mel had matching dangles in each of her nipples as well.

Men were always attracted to Mel. And she was always happy to flirt, but that's as far as it went. Mel was dead set against saving her virginity for the one man she wanted to spend the rest of her life with. So far she hadn't found him.

"We're both going to win tonight," Anna said to her reflection in the mirror.

She jumped as thunder rumbled softly in the distance. The storm would be upon them before the night was over. The air was thick with the smell of ozone and rain. It would be the first spring storm of the season. Anna only hoped it waited until she could drag Dylan to a more private place. Wet hair and runny mascara were not a good look for her.

"I hope you know what you're doing," Mel said. "Wearing that dress and beating Dylan at pool is likely to send him into cardiac arrest."

"Great," Anna said. "That's the reaction I'm looking for. My hope is that the combination of the two will put him into lust overdrive, and we can stop all this cursed foreplay and get down to the main event."

Mel laughed aloud at Anna's naivety. She had no idea how much power she had over that man. He was crazy about her.

"I think my biggest problem is going to be avoiding any wardrobe malfunctions. I feel like I'm about to pop out of this dress," Anna said, pulling the spandex down again.

The black, halter style dress left no secrets to the imagination, and she felt anything but comfortable in the contraption. The dress was like a second skin, and there was no way she could have worn underwear or a bra without every line showing.

"Well, you are," Mel said. "I'd be more worried about the gossip your father's likely to hear tomorrow when half the town sees you in that dress trying to seduce Dylan Maguire."

"Well, he told me to wear something sexy. I figure the more indecent I am the less he'll want to play pool and the more he'll want to get down to business." Anna grabbed her bag and slipped her feet into sky high heels. "Let's get out of here."

"Oh, yeah. Your dad is definitely going to hear about this," Mel said as Anna parked in the last available parking spot.

"It does look awfully busy for a Tuesday night. I didn't realize there would be so many people here."

They made their way to the big oak doors and slipped inside the crowded bar. The bass of the music thrumbed in time with the beat of her heart. Bodies moved in syncopated rhythms on the dance floor, the overheard TV's blared ESPN, and drinks were passed around heartily.

The people she'd known her whole life stopped what they were doing and gawked openly as she made her way to the bar, chin held high. Wide eyes and open mouths led way to whispers and pointed fingers until she felt the hot breath of gossip sting her ears.

Anna hated being the center of the gossip mill. She'd done her best to live a forgettable, quiet life for the last ten years, and she was about to throw it all out the window for one night of crazy sex. She'd think about the repercussions later, and she'd avoid her father in the mean time. She'd never needed a drink so bad in her life.

"Hey Brian," Anna said. "Looks like a busy night tonight. I'll have one of those," she said, pointing to the picture of the tall drink with the cherries and lemons on top. She was sure her face was tomato red, but she was going to play this scenario out if it killed her.

Brian couldn't even answer her question, the look of surprise so apparent across his face. Brian had always been a good friend to her and Mel, more like a brother to both of them.

"Are you out of your mind?" Brian hissed under his breath. "Your father is going to kill you when he hears about this. You're practically naked." He looked at Mel imploringly, trying to get her to second his opinion, but she just shrugged her shoulders at him and mouthed "I tried."

"Brian Shiney, it is no business of yours or anyone else in this town how I dress or who I date," Anna whispered back furiously.

"But you've never dressed this way before. And what did you do to your hair?"

Anna scowled at her childhood friend and prepared to blister his ears when she remembered they weren't alone in the bar.

Mr. Howard was perched on his favorite bar stool—more of a home away from home—and no one ever said there was anything wrong with his hearing. His ears were glued to the conversation just like everyone else's.

"Can I have my drink please?" Anna asked again. Brian just frowned and went off to make the concoction.

"Easy on the alcohol," Mel murmured, when she saw Anna had ordered the Long Island Iced Tea. "You want to be able to remember the greatest sex of your life."

"It looks like a fairly harmless drink," Anna said.

"How bad could it be if it has iced tea in it?"

Mel shook her head and closed her eyes. The situation could only get worse from her perspective. She took the Bud Light Brian had set on the bar for her and put the cold glass to her forehead.

"What's the matter," Anna asked.

"I just keep seeing my life flash before my eyes," Mel answered. "I've created a monster and the only person I can blame is myself. It's because I made you buy all of that sexy lingerie. It's the only explanation for why you've lost your mind."

"The only reason this is a big deal is because we're in Paradise. If we were in Dallas no one would think anything of a single young woman trying to seduce a sexy man."

"That's because everybody's crazy in the big city. It's like a rule or something," Mel said. "Mary Ann Marsdon said the last time she was in Dallas a pimp tried to sell her in the lobby of an Albertson's."

"Mary Ann Marsdon wouldn't know what the truth looked like if it hit her in the face with the broad side of a two-by-four," Anna said, rolling her eyes. "And what's that supposed to mean anyway? Are you saying I look like a prostitute?"

"No, you idiot," Mel said. "I'm your best friend, and I

just want to make sure that you won't do anything you'll regret or will embarrass you."

"I'm way past the point of embarrassment, but I'll be fine. I'm a big girl."

Brian came back with her drink and she paid the tab. "Thanks Brian. Are Dylan and Mitchell already in the back?"

He scowled at the mention of the two guys that left broken hearts trailing in a long line behind them. "Yeah, they're back there. Be careful, Anna."

*Why was everyone so worried about her?*

Dylan looked at his watch for what seemed like the hundredth time in the last fifteen minutes and took another drink of his beer. *She was late.*

"Geez, you're making me nervous and I don't even have a date," Mitchell said. "Stop fidgeting. She'll be here soon enough. Or maybe she lost her nerve and she's standing you up again."

"Thanks a lot, asshole." Dylan said.

Mitchell was right. He was acting like a virgin bride on his wedding night. He turned to look at the entrance one more time, and his jaw almost dropped to the floor. That woman could not be Anna—or maybe it could be, but he wasn't able to lift his gaze from her body to look at her face.

"Jesus Christ," Dylan said.

"Amen, brother," Mitchell answered. "This is going to be the most entertaining night I've had in a long time."

Anna came toward him with long legged strides, her hips swaying to her own song and a drink held loosely in her hand. Her hair hung in riotous curls down her back and the dress she was almost wearing clung to her curvy body like a second skin. He wanted nothing more than to lift her straight up onto a pool table and push inside her.

She came right to him and he had to lean down to hear what she was trying to say.

"What's going on, stranger?" Her voice was husky with desire and sweat popped out on his brow as she blew into his ear.

For once in his life he was completely speechless.


"Do you get the feeling we're in the way?" Mel whispered to Mitchell.

"Yeah. I feel like a voyeur. Why don't we sit on that bench, drink our beers and watch the fireworks."

"Sounds like a plan," Mel said, tapping her beer

gently to his in a toast. "Dylan doesn't happen to have a brother does he?"

Mitchell gave her an irritated glance just on principal. He didn't like for women to ask about other men when he was in their presence. "No, he doesn't have a brother. He's an only child."

"Well, it was worth asking," Mel said with a sigh. She felt that five year countdown until she was thirty clicking away.

Dylan finally got his wits about him enough to remember his name and where he was. His throat was dry as dust, but he tried to croak out the words anyway. "Are you ready to play some pool?"

"Ready as I'll ever be," Anna said, picking a cue stick off the rack and stroking its length, making Dylan groan aloud. The woman was on a mission to kill him. It was the only explanation.

"Do you know anything about nine ball?" he asked, trying to get his mind off the image of bending her over the table.

"A little bit," she purred. "They just have to go in the little holes in order, right?"

"Pretty much. Usually Mitchell and I play for money, but we don't have to bet since you're just learning."

"How about we have a different kind of bet?" Anna asked. She brought her lips up to his ear and barely touched his lobe, making him shiver at the touch. Her body brushed against his seductively and what little common sense he did have drained straight into his lap. "How about winner takes all?"

"What exactly does *all* entail?"

"Anything your imagination can think of. I kept my promise, by the way. My body is primed and ready just for you. And I'm not wearing any underwear."

"Sweet mercy." Dylan moved behind a tall bar stool to hide his obvious erection from curious onlookers and raised a brow promising retribution at Anna. She blew him a kiss and he willed the blood to go back to his brain.

"You're on, gorgeous. I never walk away from a bet where I'm sure to win. Would you like to break?"

"Oh, no. You go right ahead. I'll just stand over here and watch." She took her stance directly in his line of sight, and she sinuously trailed her fingers over the curves of her body.

Dylan found it incredibly difficult to bend over, his jeans getting tighter by the moment, but he lined up his shot and sunk a ball in the corner pocket with the break. Two more balls followed suit before he was distracted by Anna blowing on the tip of her cue stick, causing him to miscue.

"Look how many balls you got in," Anna cooed. "That's so sexy."

"You're welcome to forfeit if you don't want to take your shot. We could leave right this second."

"And what would you make me do if I lost our little bet? Take you in my mouth in the parking lot where anyone could stumble across us?"

Dylan's breathing grew rapid at the thought and he reached for her, but she quickly moved out of his grasp.

"Or maybe you'd bend me over the hood of your car and slide the hot length of you right up my ass. Hmm? Is that what you'd do?"

"Anna," he growled, coming towards her with determined strides. He couldn't have hidden his arousal even if he'd wanted to. He tossed his cue to Mitchell, determined to carry her out over his shoulder if he had to. The image of his cock buried balls deep in her ass was enough to almost make him come in his jeans.

"Uh, uh, uh," she said, shaking her finger at him. "I'm not a quitter. I'm going to finish this game. One way or the other. Now, be a good boy and have a seat."

Anna found an open shot and took her stance, leaning over the table, the tiny skirt she wore exposing an amazing length of leg that should have been illegal. Dylan whimpered in the back of his throat at the tempting picture she made, and then in the next second was growling like a junkyard dog at a man who dared to whistle at her. The man held up his hands in surrender and turned back to his own game. Mitchell's laughter in the corner earned him a dirty glare, but he couldn't take his eyes off Anna for more than a second.

But there was something different about her as she lined up her shot. The seductive temptress was gone, replaced with a face of sheer concentration. The concentration of an expert.

Her hand drew the cue stick back and let it go with an amazing amount of power. She sunk the ball she was aiming for plus one other.

"Beginner's luck," she said winking at him.

Dylan threw his head back in a roar of laughter. He'd been had by a pro. A glance at Mitchell showed that he was equally surprised by her skill. Anna made quick work of the rest of the balls and laid her cue stick on the table.

"I win. Do you know what that means?"

"What?"

"It means that your body is completely mine. To do with whatever I wish."

Dylan swallowed at the vision that popped into his mind. Anna tied to the bed, blindfolded, while he took his time pleasuring her with various toys.

I can't tell you how hot that makes me. I hope you go easy on me."

"Oh, no. I promise you things are going to be very…hard."

Dylan couldn't help himself. He tossed her over his shoulder and headed out the door. Tongues would definitely be wagging in Paradise tomorrow.

"Is it just me, or did it just get really hot in here?" Mitchell asked Mel as they were left behind to deal with the after burn.

"Yeah, well we'll see how long the sparks last before they start to fizzle. This is new territory for Anna. She's not used to dealing with men like you."

"And you are?" Mitchell asked.

*Uh, oh!* Mel recognized that particular look in a man's eyes. She wasn't naïve like Anna, and she had no wish to end up as another notch on this man's bedpost. She was a one-man kind of girl. She just hadn't found the man yet. So Mel said the first thing that came to mind.

"I'm a lesbian," she blurted out.

"Oh, really?" Mitchell asked, quirking an eyebrow. "You'd think I would have heard news about there being a lesbian in Paradise."

"Well, believe it or not, some people actually can keep secrets in this town. My girlfriend lives in Fort Worth. I just don't get to see her often." Mel lied with as straight a face as possible, but she felt the blush creeping up her neck and face.

"Huh," Mitchell said. "No offense, but you being a lesbian seems like a hell of a waste to me. You've got the kind of body a man likes to sink in to."

"So, what? Is that code for fat?"

"Hell, no. You're just a real woman. Different from the kind I usually date."

"Why, because I have a brain?"

He laughed out loud at her insult, unbothered by it. The dimples in his cheeks were threatening her resolve, but she was holding firm.

"I bet I could make you change your mind on this whole lesbian thing," he said, leaning in so his breath whispered across her cheek. "You want to give it a shot?"

Mel scooted over as far as she could, and ignored his taunting laughter. "It doesn't matter anyway. Everybody in town knows that you don't *date* anyone. I've heard cold-hearted Casey leaves your bed warm and your heart empty. And a few women have even gone so far as to say unsatisfied."

"Oh really?" Mitchell asked. "Why don't you give me

their names. I try to guarantee *all* my work."

"You know, even if I was into men, which I'm not. I wouldn't give you the time of day. I'd want someone I could depend on, someone who wanted a relationship. The person who can give me that can have my body."

Mitchell flinched involuntarily at the "R" word. Her words stung his pride, but he couldn't exactly deny the accusations.

"Seriously? You're denying yourself the pleasure of your body for a piece of paper?

"Yes," she said with such conviction that Mitchell had to stop and really look at her.

"Your holding out for a pipe dream," Mitchell said, holding her coat up for her to slip on. "You should at least enjoy the ride before you trap some poor soul into marriage."

"Someone so young shouldn't be so jaded. Maybe you should give it a try before you mock it."

"I gave it a try," Mitchell said solemnly. "And I lost everything. A piece of paper doesn't seem worth that kind of pain to me."

Mel touched her hand to his cheek before she could help herself. He didn't flinch at her touch, but he held her gaze steady, the gray of his eyes impossibly clear. And filled with so much pain and hatred that it was her that ultimately flinched.

Neither of them spoke on the long car ride home.

## CHAPTER EIGHT

"Where are we going?" Anna asked, as she took the corner that led to Baker Street like she was racing in the Indianapolis 500. She could only imagine having to explain to Sheriff Haney why she was speeding through Paradise like a bat out of hell.

*I'm sorry, Sheriff, but I'm on a mission to have the best sex of my life, and I don't have time for a ticket right now. Just stick it in my mailbox please.*

"We're headed to my place," Dylan said. "Take the first right just after my office. I live about a mile down. It's a narrow road and a little hard to see in the dark, so you might want to slow down a little." He paled as she ran through a red light and prayed they'd make it in one piece.

"Right," Anna said, her palms sweating profusely.

"How bad do we want to do this in a bed?" She took a sharp right onto the graveled road that led to Dylan's house.

"I'm thinking." He ran his fingers up and down her thigh, sending a straight shot of heat to her very core.

Her nipples were pressed prominently against the fabric of her dress, and her breathing turned to pants as he untied the string at the back of her neck and pulled the top down over her breasts. Spots danced in front of her eyes as his knuckle rubbed gently across one, and she slammed on the brakes, sending the car into a spin on the gravel.

"Christ, this is close enough. The house is just down the road. We'll get there eventually."

He got out of the car and was already on her side, unbuckling her seatbelt and pulling her out and into his arms before she could gather her wits. The night air was cool with the stormy atmosphere, but her body was a blazing inferno. Lightning now accompanied the rumbling thunder, and the storm was almost upon them. She hitched her legs around his waist as his mouth clamped around her nipple. She flung her head back in surrender and closed her eyes, the flashes of light making shapes behind her lids.

"Please, don't make me wait," she begged. "Not this time." The wind whipped her hair around her face, but it went unnoticed.

"No, baby," Dylan said, his voice husky with desire. "This time will be fast and hard. I'll be lucky to last five seconds."

"Good. I'll probably last four. Just do something before I explode. I need to feel you."

Anna's words were all the prompting he needed. Lightning shot across the sky in a jagged arch, and he saw the passion and fire moments before he devoured her mouth in a scorching kiss. He circled her round and round until they were protected under a dense copse of trees that surrounded his home. The wind whistled through the branches and thunder crashed around them, but there was only an echo of the disturbance in their subconscious as need and desire took over their bodies.

Clothes were torn and scattered as they wrestled each other to the ground. And then the rain started to fall. A torrential downpour that took them straight to the eye of the storm. Anna was oblivious to the rain. Her body was so hot she was sure that steam was rising off her skin in waves. She wrapped her legs around him and felt the head of his cock nudge her wet folds.

"Please," she begged, "Please, Dylan."

"Tell me what you want," he said, whispering in her ear. He ran his hands over her body, branding her lush curves with his touch. He pushed inside her slightly and then pulled away, causing her to moan in frustration.

"I want you inside of me," she screamed. "Do it!"

Dylan plunged into her waiting heat without any warning, causing her to scream in a mix of pain and pleasure. Her sheath was achingly tight, but she adjusted quickly to his size, accepting him fully. He didn't stop to let her catch her breath but pushed her until she was blinded by the feelings roiling inside her. All she could do was hang on for the ride.

"More," he demanded. "I want more." He quickened his pace, sending Anna's body into a spiraling vortex of eruptions. He stiffened above her and swelled within her tight sheath. The explosion of his come filled her to bursting and sent her into another fit of rapture.

"Am I still alive?" Anna asked a few moments or hours later. She wasn't sure which. The only reason she was brought back from semi-unconsciousness was because she was starting to drown.

"Mmm," Dylan said in response.

*Sure, easy for him. He's on top.* "Ah, Dylan," she said. "I'm having kind of a problem here."

He lifted his head and looked at her in disgust. "Geez, woman, haven't you ever heard of afterglow?"

"Excuse me?" she said. "You happen to be crushing me into the ground. Where, I might add, a rock has made itself at home in my right butt cheek. Not to mention the fact that I'm drowning."

"Oh," he said, laughing and causing another tingle to surface in her nether-region. "Is this better?" he asked, flipping their positions so she was on top. She looked like an ethereal creature from the sea. Her head lifted high and her hair hanging in wet ropes.

"Ahh, this is much better, but do you think we might get to go inside soon? I've never been much for the great outdoors," she said, tracing her fingers along the lines of his face.

He really was a beautiful man. The sharp angles of his face sported a five o'clock shadow and raindrops clung to his lashes. She leaned down gently and took his bottom lip in her mouth, sucking gently. She could feel his body stir beneath hers and knew that she would always remember this moment, the rain falling quietly now and the look of what she wished was love in his eyes. Memories were all she needed.

"I think the great outdoors agree with you quite well," Dylan said, seeing the shuttered look come into her eyes. She was thinking again, and it was too early in their affair to have such heavy thoughts. He was doing his damnedest to block his own thoughts from coming to the surface.

Anna Hollis was going to be a complication that could change his life forever. He just had to figure out if he wanted to let her. "How does a hot shower sound?"

"I don't know. Do I have to take one alone?"

"Absolutely not," Dylan said, sitting up with her still on his lap. "That wouldn't be any way to treat a guest." He stood up slowly, making sure his legs would support him, and swung Anna up into his arms.

"Oh my God. Please don't drop me."

"Are you questioning my manhood?" He relaxed his arms so she started to fall and had to wrap her arms around his neck to hang on.

"No," she said. "You're very manly and tough. And this is very romantic. What about our clothes?"

"We're not going to need them for a while."

"No, you idiot," Anna said, laughing. "Our clothes are all over your front yard. What if someone drives up?"

"Then they're bound to get an education."

She buried her face in his neck, inhaling the scent of male and rain and feeling the walls she guarded so fiercely around her heart begin to crack. *Snap out of it, Anna. No matter what you feel, Dylan Maguire will never feel the same way about you.*

As they made their way up the wooden steps that led to Dylan's front porch, Anna looked around at the outside of his home for the first time since they'd arrived. At first glance, it looked like an average cabin in the woods. At second glance, it was a majestic display of wood and angles, a cross between Frank Lloyd Wright and Paul Bunyan's cabin.

"Wow," Anna said. "This is some place you've got here."

"It's just a place to live," Dylan said, uncomfortable at her scrutiny. "I've always felt it's too big for one person, but it's comfortable."

Anna was one of the few people that had seen his home. It had been a sanctuary to him after his divorce, a place he could find the solitude he needed in his busy life. "Can you get the door?" he asked, shifting her in his arms.

"Well I can't wait to get the tour," she told him. "Much, much later."

"I believe we have a date in the shower." He set her down gently and encircled her in his arms loosely, kissing her lips softly and gently nibbling his way down to her neck.

"Mmm," Anna groaned. "You are so good at that."

"You haven't seen the half of it yet," he said, biting her earlobe. He backed her towards the master suite, guiding her with the touch of his body. "This is my bedroom."

"It's beautiful," Anna said, never taking her eyes off his. "Are we close to the shower?"

"It's right here. And it's plenty big enough for what I have in mind."

"That sounds like boasting. You must have something to prove," she said, grasping his rapidly returning hardness in her hands.

"I guess I do." He pushed her into the shower and adjusted the nozzle before turning on the water. "Constructive criticism is greatly appreciated."

He skimmed his finger across her nipple and pinched lightly, causing her to draw in a sharp breath. "You like that?"

"Yes," she hissed.

"Then we'll experiment more with it later. I've got a terrible thirst for you." His fingers found their way to her pussy, flicking the tight swollen bud buried in her folds. Her fingernails raked his shoulders as he pushed two fingers inside of her.

"You're so tight. You fit like a glove around my cock."

"Prove it."

He pushed her against the tile wall and propped her leg over his arm, opening her to his invasion. He slid home smoothly and rocked them both to oblivion.

Dylan woke three hours later to the sound of a car engine starting. He reached out and felt the cool sheets next to him and knew that Anna was gone. He sat up slowly and rubbed his hands over his face before walking naked to the front door. He saw the red flash of her taillights before she turned off the long graveled road, he assumed, headed toward home.

It was what he wanted. What they both agreed on. Two ships passing in the night. And if the spot just under his heart hurt a little, he had no one to blame but himself.

"Shit," he yelled, punching his fist against the wall. He'd never been on the receiving end of being left in the middle of the night. He was the one who was supposed to leave, or the one who said it's time for you to go.

Even now he wanted her again. No, needed her again. His dick was hard again, and images of her bent over his bed, sucking his cock or his face buried in her pussy bombarded his mind. But now she was gone. He thought she'd drained him dry in the few hours of lovemaking they'd had together. She was like a drug he couldn't get out of his system.

"She can run, but she can't hide," Dylan said to the empty room. He stroked his cock, picturing her tight lips around it, until his seed spurted into his waiting hand. Anna Hollis wasn't going to slip out of his grasp so easily.

## CHAPTER NINE

Anna drove into Paradise with her eyes wide open, trying to see the town through a stranger's viewpoint. That's what she felt like. A stranger. It had been two long weeks since she'd laid eyes on the place, and she wasn't sure another week or two wouldn't do her any good. Two long weeks since she'd seen Dylan.

She was a coward, plain and simple. As soon as she'd left his bed, she'd packed all her things in a suitcase, written her father a note explaining that she was gone to check on all the Hollis stores, and run as far and fast as she could. But she was back and ready to face her fears. Sort of.

She pulled into a parking spot in front of *Buy the Book*, Mel's bookstore, and finger combed her hair. She'd left the top down on her car and instead of looking sexy and tousled as she'd hoped, she looked like she just rolled out of bed. She refreshed her lipstick and pushed her sunglasses on the top of her head in hopes that no one would notice.

Anna had always enjoyed walking into the bookstore, the smell of the pages and glue that had led her to so many peaceful hours, fresh coffee and sandwiches being served in the café and the tinkle of bells as customers walked in and out.

She inhaled the homey aroma and looked around to see if anything had changed in the past weeks. The place was crowded with people browsing the shelves or study groups lounging in the overstuffed chairs in the corner. She saw the store manager and a couple of other full time employees, looking frazzled and helping as many people as possible at the same time.

Anna headed to the back of the store to the café in hopes of finding Mel reasonably unattached. Mel was behind the counter taking inventory of all the food supplies, her hair sticking up in all directions, more so than usual, and a pencil stuck behind each ear.

"Wow, you guys are packed," Anna said.

Mel looked up, startled at Anna's appearance after being gone so long. "Ah, so the prodigal daughter returns," she said, smiling. "I was wondering if you were ever going to come back. I was planning on moving my stuff into your house when it was finished, but I guess I'll have to stay in my own meager dwelling.

"Shut up," Anna said by way of greeting. "So, I hear you're a lesbian."

"Which is why we're so busy today," Mel said, running her fingers through her hair, explaining the dishevelment.

"Everyone has stopped by at one point or another to get a look at me, like I've sprouted wings or had the word "lesbian" tattooed on my forehead. I've had everything from disdainful glances to people wanting me to describe my sex life in lurid detail. Of course, I've never had any kind of sex life before, so I'm a little short on a lot of the details. Oh, and Mrs. Neagley winked at me, which kind of grossed me out, but explains why she's spent so many years going to garage sells with Erma Miller."

"Well, I guess I can look on the bright side," Anna said smiling. "Everyone's probably so busy talking about you that maybe they've forgotten all about me."

"Yeah, tell me about it. I've been dodging phone calls from my mother for weeks. Getting gossip about her own daughter doesn't make the activity quite as fun as spreading it about other people's kids. And besides, you're the one that said you wanted to be so wild that the women gossip about you in the beauty salon. Go out and do something stupid again so the spotlight will be off me."

"With the way things have been going lately, it'll only be a matter of time."

Mel nodded toward the window where a group of children was standing with their faces pressed against the glass. "On the upside, though, business has been great. Where'd you hear the news?"

"I stopped in the bank on my way here," Anna said, barely able to contain her laughter at the hilarity of it all. "Barbara Rubenstein stopped me at the counter and wanted to know if I'd always known you were a lesbian or if I was just as surprised as the rest of the town when you came out of the closet."

"I shudder to think what you told her." Mel closed her eyes in dread.

"I told her I've always known, but I respected your privacy."

"Ohmigod," Mel said. "This just keeps getting better."

"Just kidding. I gave my best blank face and told her I had no idea what she was talking about. I used my rich, haughty girl voice, and threatened to take all my money out of the bank if she started spreading rumors."

"Damn, Della Samuels," Mel muttered. "I hope all the chemicals that woman uses on her hair makes her pubic hair fall out."

"Ouch," Anna said. "That's harsh."

"Well, the woman has spread it all over town that

I'm a lesbian," Mel whined. "Now I'm never going to find my soul mate."

"Yeah, but wishing someone's pubic hairs to fall out is like a cardinal sin or something," Anna said, biting her lip. "You can get all kinds of bad Karma for a wish like that. Why did she start spreading the rumor anyway?"

"Well, I kind of told Mitchell that I was a lesbian so he'd stop looking at me like I was little red riding hood and he was the big bad wolf. I don't have the death wish that you do when it comes to men. I want a nice, sensible guy. Maybe a banker or a produce guy at the supermarket."

"Oscar Daniels works in the produce section at Howard's Grocery," Anna said, a look of utter disgust on her face. "Everyone in town knows he doesn't wash his hands after he uses the restroom. Brian said he saw him walk into a stall and leave without even rinsing. In a stall! You know what that means."

"I didn't say I wanted to marry Oscar Daniels for Pete's sake," Mel said in exasperation. "I just want someone who's reliable and will treat me like a queen for the rest of my life. You're missing the point here. I was leading up to your situation, which since you're standing here interrupting my work day, I assume you've decided to face the consequences of your actions?"

"Well, I really came back because I didn't have anywhere else left to go," Anna said depressed. "I've been to every *Hollis Tools* store in the state of Texas, and I have no place else to turn. So am I ready to face the consequences? The answer is no, but I don't really have any other choice."

Anna sat on a stool at the counter and laid her head down on the cool surface. "Have you seen him," she mumbled in Mel's general direction.

"I'm sorry?" Mel asked, knowing exactly what Anna wanted to know. "I don't think I heard you correctly."

"You heard me," Anna said, humiliated beyond all belief. "How does he look? Was he mad?"

"Oh, he looks as good as ever," Mel said. "Was he mad? I'm not really sure if mad describes it. From what I hear around town, he's been disgruntled at best and a complete asshole at worst. I'll let you find out for yourself. It won't be long before word hits that you're back in town."

"I shouldn't have left so soon," Anna said.

"You think?" Mel asked sarcastically. "It could be for the best though. Maybe it'll give him a taste of his own medicine. He's usually the one that walks out in the middle of the night and never looks back. I just don't think you should get into the habit of it."

"I think I've made a huge miscalculation," Anna said, pounding her forehead on the countertop.

"Stop doing that," Mel hissed. "I don't need any more strange looks."

"He's like an addiction," Anna continued. "I don't think I'll ever get enough of him. That's the real reason I ran away. He's ruined me for all other men."

"Wow. That's impressive to hit a ten on the scale your first time out. I'm only shooting for an eight or an eight plus. That way I always know I haven't capped out. And look on the bright side," Mel said. "At least you've had a man. You're an expert compared to me."

"Thanks," Anna said, "I think. I've got to protect myself, Mel. What if I keep seeing him and end up falling for him? Dylan Maguire will never love any one woman. I just don't know what to do."

"Sometimes you just have to take chances," Mel said. "It's all a crap shoot. So what are you going to do?"

"I'm going to walk down to Norma's Bakery and buy as much chocolate as possible, and then I'm going to go home and eat every bit of it," Anna said. "You want to come over tonight and share it with me?"

"I can't," Mel said. "I'm closing the store tonight, and then I'm going home and soaking in the hot tub." She had a feeling that Anna wouldn't be as free as she thought she would later on.

"I guess I'll catch you later," Anna said, heading

towards the door. "Chocolate cream pie just became a huge priority."

"Understandable," Mel said, waving her out the door.

"Oh, by the way," Anna yelled across the room, "thanks for taking care of any problems on the house."

No problem, Mel thought, tormented. I've only had to spend every day with Mitchell for the last two weeks. No problem at all. Of course, he was now on a mission to prove that she wasn't a lesbian, but fortunately she had a will power of iron and was able to thwart his feeble attempts at seduction.

Anna made her way through the crowd and back to the sidewalk. It was a beautiful day, the trees and flowers blooming and the sun shining.

She waved to several people as she headed to Norma's and knew they were curious about her and Dylan. The speculative glances were grating on her nerves. Their relationship had turned out to be a car wreck, it was almost impossible not to watch how the events played out.

She could never pass Norma's without wanting to stop in a buy something. The glass window in front boasted rows of pies, tarts and cookies, and *Norma's Bakery* was painted in discreet gold letters at the bottom of the window.

She opened the door and welcomed the smell that greeted her. The place was full at the lunch hour, and there wasn't an open table anywhere in sight.

"Hi, Norma," Anna said. "Everything looks great today."

"Well, it's fresh like always," she said, her mouth turned down into a permanent scowl.

Anna had no idea how the woman had stayed in business for forty years. Her disposition wasn't nearly as sweet as the desserts she made.

"I'll take a chocolate cream pie and a dozen double fudge brownies." She kept a smile glued to her face despite Norma's peevishness.

"You want the whole pie?" Norma asked with a quick glance to Anna's middle.

Anna colored slightly at the insinuation and remembered with clarity that Norma might have reason to suspect. *How could she be so stupid?* They'd made love countless times without one thought of protection entering their minds. The smell of the sweets made the bile rise in her throat, but she choked it down. "Yes. I need the whole pie. Dad wanted me to pick one up for dessert tonight," she lied easily.

She felt the prickle on the back of her neck moments after silence descended over the bakery. She was determined not to turn around, sure that ignorance was bliss in this case. She shifted slightly so she could see her reflection in the glass cases next to the counter. She gasped as she saw Dylan behind her, entirely too close for comfort.

"Excuse me, Norma," Anna said. "I'm going to use the restroom. Go ahead and charge it to the store's account and box them up for me." Businesses all over town still worked on a credit system, just the way it had always been since the town's creation.

Anna kept her gaze straight ahead, never acknowledging Dylan's appearance, and headed towards the bathroom at top speed, praying that he'd be gone when she came out. She turned the handle and felt a hand at the small of her back, nudging her none so gently.

"What are you doing?" she asked as she turned and tried to push Dylan out of the bathroom. "Are you out of your mind? Is there not enough gossip about the two of us to satisfy you?"

"I believe the only person to blame for gossip is yourself sweetheart," he said, lifting her across the threshold and shutting the bathroom door.

The last thing Anna saw were dozens of faces in complete shock, the gasp that went through the crowd deafening in her ears. Couples just did not go into restrooms together. She hadn't been back in Paradise an hour and already the gossip mill had ammunition.

"I'll never be able to show my face in this town again," she cried. "Are you happy now?"

"I haven't been happy in two weeks. Where the hell did you run of to?" He hadn't meant to sound so desperate. Angry and irritated, yes, but not desperate.

"I had to go," Anna said, tired of the turmoil she felt in the pit of her stomach every time he was near. "I'm not cut out for this, Dylan. I thought I could be brave and do something I missed out on for the past several years, but I can't. I'm not built for relationships, or I guess more aptly, one night stands. They just aren't for me, and Lord knows that you definitely aren't built for relationships." She laid her head down on his chest in defeat.

"Are you finished?" he asked, tracing his finger over her lips to quiet her protests. "I think there's more to you than you give yourself credit for. I think there's more to both of us."

"I don't know what you mean." She'd given up the pretense of trying to push him away and melted into his arms. He was massaging her scalp with one hand and rubbing her lower back with the other, both soothing gestures.

"I mean that I think we should start over and go in a different direction. Why don't I take you to dinner tonight? You can wear something sexy and I'll even put on a tie."

"Does starting over in a new direction mean no sex?"

"Hell no, but I would have grudgingly gone along with the idea if you'd wanted me to."

"I guess I could go on a date with you," she said, running her palms over his chest. "I just want you to understand that I'm trying to protect myself. I could fall in love with you if I'm not careful."

Anna lifted up on her toes and kissed him lightly on the lips. "Oh, and by the way, I just realized that neither of us used protection the last time we made love. Chances are I'm not pregnant, but maybe you want to pick up a box of condoms before our next encounter."

Dylan had paled at her words and then turned an odd shade of green.

"Oh, and for God's sake, don't buy them at Wall's Pharmacy. June Wall will tell everyone in town just what you bought as soon as you walk out the door. Did you know the Mayor orders a case of Viagra every six months?"

Dylan choked at the thought of the little round man that resembled Danny DeVito, and what he could possibly do with a case of Viagra, but Anna's previous word's still left him in shock. *Pregnant.*

Anna nudged Dylan out of the way while he was still speechless. She lifted her chin high and opened the bathroom door. Not one person had moved since they'd gone in together, and if she had to guess, several people had come in after being informed of the situation and decided to stay around to see what happened.

She gathered her desserts and her courage and left the crowd to gossip in the bakery. Somehow she had to buy a pregnancy test without everybody in the whole county finding out.

Dylan headed out at his own pace, unbothered by the stares and whispers, his mind on what she'd said. *Love. Pregnancy.* He was afraid, but he found there was a yearning in him he didn't know he harbored. Things were moving faster than he wanted, but he didn't have a choice because he was already in love with Anna Hollis.

## CHAPTER TEN

*Ahh. . .Home sweet home.*

Anna looked at the Hollis Mansion from the end of the long driveway and smiled wistfully. It was home and always would be, no matter how long she was gone.

Cherry trees lined the long driveway and the pink blossoms were blooming in full glory. Weeping Willows flanked each corner of the house and a white swing hung from one of the branches. Everything was so green and pure.

She drove down the long driveway and felt like the princess of the castle as pink blossoms reigned down on her. Her smile brightened at the sight of her father as he closed the screen door behind him and waited for her arrival on the wide, columned front porch, but it dimmed slightly as she saw his expression. He was not happy to see her from the looks of things. She'd have to guess by the deep set frown lines that word had already reached his ears about the bathroom incident. And then fear gripped her heart. What if someone had seen her walk into the Walgreens two towns away? She clutched the plastic bag that held the home pregnancy kit in her hand and then hurriedly shoved it into her handbag. She was prepared to lie like crazy just in case.

Anna took her time pulling the luggage out of her trunk, stalling the upcoming confrontation as long as possible.

"Hi, Dad," she said, walking past him in hopes that she could make it to her rooms without a confrontation.

"Don't you hi, Dad me," he said, hot on her trail. "Do you have any idea the number of phone calls I've gotten today? And it's only the middle of the afternoon."

"I'm twenty-five years old. I shouldn't have to explain my actions to the whole town or be under their scrutiny twenty-four hours a day."

"That's the price you pay when you live in a small town. You know this, so why would you deliberately do something to cause such a ruckus?"

"I didn't *do* anything. It was all Dylan's fault. He pushed me into the bathroom. I couldn't stop him."

"What are you talking about? What bathroom?" Jack

asked, confused.

"Well, what are you talking about?" Anna asked, wishing she could drop off the planet. Surely someone had called to tell him about the bathroom incident. She kept her fingers crossed about Walgreens.

"I'm talking about fifty people calling me wanting to know if I knew you were back in town. They said you came rolling into town like you didn't have a care in the world. Not that you let me know of your comings and goings. And Mrs. Edgars wanted to know why you felt like you didn't have to obey traffic laws."

"I obeyed all traffic laws, dad. Mrs. Edgars is a hundred and forty years old. She couldn't see a stop sign if it was five feet in front of her."

He nodded his head in partial agreement. Anna noticed the look on his face hadn't changed, but when she examined it closer, she realized it wasn't anger that cause the lines to furrow his brow. It was sadness, and worse, disappointment.

"I'm sorry, Dad. I should have called to let you know when I was getting back into town. I didn't mean to make you worry," she said, pulling him into a hug. "I probably should have given you more detail as to why I was leaving as well, but I didn't think I could explain it at the time without breaking down. I just needed to leave town."

"Was it because of Dylan?" he asked, concerned.

"Yes, but I think I have everything under control now."

"What did he do?" Jack demanded. "I'll take the hide off that boy if he's done anything to hurt you. I told him before he even asked you out to make sure he took care of you."

"What?"

Jack realized his blunder too late. "Umm. . .It's not what it seems Anna. I was just worried about you being cooped up in the house all the time. I wanted you to be happy, to find a man you could settle down with and raise a family."

"You set this all up?" she asked, mortified. "I'll never be able to face him again. He must think I'm the most desperate woman in the world to have my father set up my dates for me."

"It's not like that Anna. Settle down. Dylan asked about you first. It was after he mentioned you that I started to get the idea in my head. Lord knows the both of you are attracted to each other. I watched you circle around it for months before either of you made a move."

Anna closed her eyes in embarrassment. Apparently she hadn't hidden her lustful gazes well enough for her father not to notice. "Why didn't he tell me?" she asked.

"Why would he?" Jack countered. "It's not as big of a

deal as you're making it out to be. You like him, he likes you, end of story."

"It's not like it matters anyway," she said. "I hate to disappoint you, but my relationship with Dylan is nothing more than superficial. I never want to get married or have a family."

Anna blanched at the thought that she might be carrying Dylan's child even as she spoke the denial to her father, and the feeling didn't scare her as much as it should have. In fact, the more she thought about it, the more she adjusted to the idea, but she squashed the feeling before she could become too comfortable.

"How could you even want that for me after what you went through when mom died?"

"What nonsense. You're telling me you'd give up a lifetime of happiness with a man you loved and the joy of having children because you're afraid. That doesn't sound like the Anna Hollis I know."

"Well it's the only Anna Hollis there is, and I never said I loved him."

"Let me tell you something young lady. That is a foolish notion and hopefully you'll come to your senses soon. I wouldn't trade one moment of the time I got to spend with your mother. Even if I'd known our time together was going to be short I'd have married her anyway and cherished our time as much as I still do. You make your own happiness, Anna, and live the hand life deals you." He casually brushed the tears off his cheek with a shaky hand.

"I'm sorry, Dad. I didn't mean to make you sad. I'm just scared. I don't think I could bear to lose someone I loved that much. I don't think I'm as strong as you are."

"Nonsense. You have Hollis blood in you veins, don't you? Just think about what I said. I know you'll make the right decision when the time comes. Now what's this about a bathroom incident?"

Anna blushed at the thought of what he was bound to find out at any moment. "I think I'll plead the Fifth on this one and let you find out from your next caller. I don't think I can handle any more embarrassing situations today."

"Well that sounds promising. I think I'll go wait next to the phone just in case. Is there anything else you need to tell me about?"

"No," Anna winced at the lie. Somehow parents always knew when their kids were hiding things from them.

Anna gave him a backwards wave and headed upstairs to get ready for an evening with Dylan. Not just a hot night of sex, though hopefully that would be included, but an actual date where they could sit face to face and see if they had anything in common besides a sizzling attraction. Talk about scary. What if they sat in complete silence the entire meal and just stared at each other?

"Well, there's only one way to find out," she said to herself. She pulled a dress out of the closet and ran her bathwater, sprinkling in the scented sea salts Mel had given her for her birthday. The lilac aroma rose fragrantly in a cloud of steam as she stepped into the hot water.

She looked at the little white box in front of her. "Well it's now or never," she said, pulling the test out of the box.

The directions said she had to wait three minutes before accurate results would be displayed, so she laid the test on the counter and hopped in the tub, so she wouldn't be biting her fingernails for the next three minutes.

Anna leaned her head back and closed her eyes, letting her muscles relax from the long car ride.

And then the phone rang. . .and rang. . .and rang.

"Dammit. Can't I have five minutes of peace and quiet?" she yelled to no one in particular.

It could only be a select few who were calling. She only gave her number to close friends or family. It would just have to wait, whatever *it* was.

The mood broken, she bathed quickly and stepped out of the tub. She closed her eyes and picked up the test and then cracked one eye to see what the results were.

"Oh." Relief and a little disappointment coursed through her as she saw the negative sign in the box. It wasn't meant to be.

She wrapped herself in a thick towel, looking frantically at the clock as she began pulling undergarments out of drawers. It was later than she'd thought. Dylan would be there before she knew it.

She did a light makeup job, since it was so warm outside, and highlighted her eyes with a touch of shadow. She dusted her face and shoulders with a shimmery powder and pulled her hair up in a high pony tail on her head to keep the thick mass off the back of her neck. Summer was just around the corner, and with the hot spring days they'd been having, she couldn't imagine what the heat in the summer was going to be like.

The stockings she had laid out on the bed already looked suffocating, so she chose to go without them for the evening. She didn't need them, her legs being one of her best features, long, tanned and smooth. It's not like they would stay on long anyway.

Anna winced as she heard the phone warble from inside her purse once again. "Fine, I'm coming. I'm coming," she said, throwing her hands up in the air and hurrying over to the front entry table in her suite, only wearing her underwear and high heels.

Her heel snagged the carpet runner in the foyer and she went sprawling in a heap on the floor. She barely managed to get her fingers around her purse when she crash landed, and her phone ended up falling on her forehead to add insult to injury.

"Holy cow." She tried to get her breath back and thanked God that no one had been around to see her make a fool of herself. She felt all her extremities to make sure nothing was hurt, other than her pride, and picked up her phone since it continued to play Hungarian Rhapsody in shrill tones.

"What," she said into the receiver. She pulled herself up slowly and sat in the small Queen Anne chair next to the table.

"Is this Anna Hollis?" the voice on the other asked.

She could barely understand the question, the voice was so low and distorted. "This is Anna. Who is this?"

"That's not important. All you need to know is that you'd better stay away from Dylan Maguire or the next time you pass over Paradise Crossing I'll make sure you end up on the rocks below. Is that understood?"

Fear gripped Anna's heart in a suffocating vise, and the color drained from her face. Someone was actually threatening to kill her. Anger quickly replaced fear, that someone would dare to threaten her over something as silly as who she dated.

"How dare you threaten me," Anna yelled into the phone. "I guess you'd better give it your best shot because I'm going to keep seeing Dylan you jealous freak. And you know what? There's nothing in this world you could threaten me with to make me give up the best sex of my life. You must be out of your mind."

Anna pulled the phone back from her ear slightly as it slammed down on the other end. Her adrenaline was pumping full steam ahead and she felt invigorated.

*She was a moron.* She'd just taunted a madman to come and kill her because she wasn't willing to give up sex. But it felt great to stand up for herself. It had been too long since she'd gotten to do that.

"I've had enough of this," Anna said, dialing her phone. Relief coursed through her when the person she was looking for picked up on the other end.

"Sheriff Haney? This is Anna Hollis." She listened for a few seconds before she felt the flush in her cheeks. "No, I wasn't breaking any traffic laws. I promise."

Damn Mrs. Edgars, the old busybody, Anna thought sourly. All she had to do all day was sit on her front porch and spy on the citizens of Paradise. She should get a citation for butting into other people's business.

She dropped her head on her knees with Sheriff Haney's next statement. "No, I didn't know it was considered public indecency to go into a woman's restroom with a man."

She listened to the set down in acceptance. There wasn't really a whole lot she could do when the Sheriff was scolding her.

"No, Sheriff Haney. I won't do it again."

"No, sir. . .Well it wasn't really my fault. Dylan forced his way in." Her efforts to clear her name fell on deaf ears. She'd apparently been labeled a Jezebel by the entire town.

"Sheriff Haney," Anna interrupted. "I've actually called for a different reason. You see, someone keeps threatening me, and I just got another phone call. I'd appreciate it if you take a statement so I can get everything documented."

"Thank you, sir. I appreciate it."

Anna hung up the phone and put her head down on the table. Why did things like this happen to her? She thought about it for a moment and realized things like that never happened to her when she was a shy nobody. Maybe that was the key.

"Well it's too late for all that now," she said, getting up to get dressed before the Sheriff arrived. She pulled on the strapless sheath of turquoise silk and looked at herself in the mirror. The dress was perfect, stopping mid-thigh, and the exact shade of her eyes. It was sure to knock

Dylan dead.

"Okay bad choice of words," she muttered, grabbing her shawl and matching handbag. Sheriff Haney would be there any minute and she wanted to get the interview over with before Dylan showed up.

"Well don't you look pretty," her father said as she came down the stairs.

"Thanks. How's phone duty going? Have you heard anything new?" she asked, crossing her fingers that her name had stayed clear of the lines.

"Nothing about you. Yet," he amended. "It must be pretty bad for people to be afraid to call and tell me, but I'll find out eventually."

"That's what I'm afraid of," Anna muttered.

"I heard that."

"You always do. I'm going out to dinner tonight with Dylan, so I probably won't be home if you do get a call."

"Well, maybe folks have forgotten about you with all the happenings today. I think the heat is starting to affect people's minds," Jack said. "The Shiney's have a new grandbaby, and I'm sure I'll go by for a pint or two tonight to help them celebrate. I think Brian's brother is bound and determined to populate the world. This will be their fifth."

"Maybe he's just trying to make up for Brian not having any," Anna said.

"Brian's been sweet on Veronica Fox since high school. He'll eventually find his way out of the paper bag he lives in and ask her out."

"Brian. . .likes Veronica?" Anna stuttered. "How do you know these things? He's never said a word about her to me or Mel."

"Well, I happen to be a great observer of people. It comes with running a business for so long. Douglas Howard called a few minutes ago to tell me that Norma's son was arrested again for stealing a case of Bud Light from a 7-Eleven. No wonder she's always in a bad mood. The boy just as easily could have taken one of the cases she keeps in her refrigerator and not gone to jail for it. I've always suspected that Norma's first husband was her second cousin, but no one knows for sure."

Anna crinkled her nose. "Ughh."  But that put more light on Norma's sour disposition.

She checked the time once again. Where was Sheriff Haney? She didn't have all day to wait on him. What did he think her tax dollars were paid for?

She heard a car door slam and took back her bad thoughts of the man. She kissed her dad on the cheek, told him bye and walked quickly to the door, hoping to head off the Sheriff at the front porch. The last thing she wanted was to worry her dad, and she would make it clear to the Sheriff that she didn't want him finding out about the threats.

"Thanks for coming Sheriff," Anna said by way of greeting. She led him to a white wicker chair and sat down beside him.

"Now what's all this about threats?" he asked, clearly disbelieving of her tale.

Anna had just opened her mouth to speak when she noticed the snappy little car coming up her driveway. Her mouth dropped open at the sight of the black Aston Martin, and a bubble of envy formed in the pit of her stomach. That was one sexy car, and she didn't know anyone in Paradise who owned one.

Sheriff Haney was equally stunned by the machine, but nothing could have hidden their surprise at who stepped out of the driver's side.

"That's your car?" Anna asked Dylan as he slowly made his way up the wide front steps. She didn't notice the expensive Italian suit he wore that made him devastatingly handsome or the yellow roses he held in his hand.

"Yeah, do you like it?" he asked, smiling at her reaction.

"Is it a V-12?" Anna asked, wanting nothing more

than to run her fingers over every inch of the car.

"Of course. I didn't know you were into cars?"

"Are you kidding me? My grandfather taught me how to rebuild an engine when I was in high school. I wanted to be a mechanic until I realized it wouldn't help me run Hollis Tools one day."

Dylan looked over and finally noticed the Sheriff standing next to Anna. "Good afternoon, Sheriff. What brings you out here?"

"Well, I was actually just asking that question myself when you drove up. I take it you two are headed out tonight?"

"We don't have reservations until seven thirty, so there's no rush," Dylan said. He could tell by the way Anna was avoiding his eyes she didn't want him to know why she'd called the sheriff, but it was too bad because he wasn't going to budge.

"Now Anna, tell me again about these threats you're getting," the sheriff continued.

"You got another one?" Dylan asked.

"Yes, but this time it wasn't a note. They got my private cell number and called me. I'll start at the beginning sheriff," Anna said, sitting next to Dylan.

"I received the first note a little over three weeks

ago, when Dylan and I first met. I found this note under my windshield wipers when I left Dylan's office," she said handing him the slightly crumpled note.

Sheriff Haney read the note and shook his head. "Looks to me like someone doesn't want you two to see each other. What were you doing at Dylan's office that day if you'd just met?"

Anna colored slightly, remembering exactly what they'd been doing at their first meeting. She cleared her throat and said, "Dylan's building my house for me. I was there for the preliminary meeting."

"Hmm. . ." Sheriff Haney said, "I heard you were moving out. I drove by there a few days ago. Looks like it's going to be a grand place."

She made a noncommittal sound in her throat because the truth was, she hadn't laid eyes on the place since they'd broken ground. She'd let Mel handle anything that came up just to avoid Dylan.

Everything in Paradise moved slow, conversations, courtships and investigations included. It was the way of a small southern town, only Anna was tired of moving slow.

"Then what happened?" the sheriff asked when he realized he wasn't going to get any interesting gossip from Anna.

"Well, that same day on my way home a black sedan

tried to run me off Hollis Bridge. It came right up on my back fender and then came around to the side really fast. The windows were tinted dark, so I couldn't see who was driving. They kept swerving closer, so I slammed on my brakes and turned hard. I barely stopped skidding before I was on the edge of the bridge. One more inch and I would have gone over. By the time I looked up the car was too far down the road for me to see a license plate."

"Why didn't you report the incident then?" Sheriff Haney asked.

"After it happened, I decided that I wasn't going to see Dylan anymore. I didn't think anything else would happen."

Dylan snorted at the reminder that she'd run from him.

"Looks to me like you changed your mind," the sheriff said.

"I was persuaded to change my mind," Anna said, smiling at Dylan. "I've been out of town for a while and I haven't received anything else until today."

"You said you received a call on your cell phone," Sheriff Haney said. "What did they say?"

"They just said that if I didn't stay away from Dylan the next time they'd make sure I ended up in at the bottom of the river."

"Did you recognize the voice?"

"No, I couldn't even tell if it was a man or a woman. The voice was deep and gravelly."

"What was your response? Were you able to get them to say anything else that might jog a memory or recognition of the voice?"

"Umm. . .No not really," Anna stuttered. "I might have made whoever it was a little upset. They slammed the phone down in my ear."

"What did you say?" Dylan asked, his face a mask of disbelief and anger.

"Basically, I said I wasn't going to stop seeing you. I might not have used those exact words though."

Both men had identical expressions on their face. Apparently, the consensus was she was an idiot, much like the conclusion she'd come to herself after hanging up the phone.

"Would you mind if I took your cell phone in?" the sheriff asked. "There are things we can do to retrieve the number. Maybe we'll get lucky. In the meantime, be careful. You should have come to me before. You might also see if the two of you can come up with someone who could be doing this."

"We'll do the best we can. Thanks for coming out Sheriff Haney," Anna said, shaking his hand. "Oh, and sheriff, I'd like to keep this just between us. I don't want my father to worry."

He grunted in what seemed like ascent and turned to Dylan. "Dylan, you had a little trouble with a fire around the same time Anna started getting threats. Could be both of you need to be on your guard."

"I didn't think the incidents were related at the time, but I'll keep an eye out," Dylan told him.

"Oh, and Anna" the sheriff said before getting into his cruiser, "Let's try to keep from causing any more public disturbances in the middle of town. You haven't been back more than a few hours and my phone's been ringing off the hook about you all afternoon. I don't know how your father puts up with the stress."

"Shut up," Anna said to Dylan when he started to laugh. "It was all your fault and your name never comes up when people are dealing out the blame."

"What can I say? The public loves me," he said getting his first real look at her outfit. He let out a long wolf whistle and looked over the length of her. "You look amazing."

"You don't look so bad yourself. I have to say that a suit and tie agrees with you."

"Well, I didn't always work in Paradise you know," he said leading her to his car.

"No, I didn't know," she said. "Which I guess is the point of this date, isn't it?"

"Partly," he said with a lascivious wink. He threw a box of seventy-two condoms in her lap, making her roar with laughter.

"My, don't we have high aspirations," Anna said, putting them back in his bag.

"I take it our past mistakes have been overlooked?" Dylan asked, referring to their previous trysts without the aid of a condom.

"Everything's great," Anna said.

The silence lapsed as the made their way out of Paradise, both thinking private but similar thoughts. Would love be easier for them to grasp with a child involved?

"Hopefully, we'll find out a little bit about each other on this outing," Dylan said, breaking the ice. "I already know that you love cars, which I might add happens to be a love of mine as well. You made a good choice when you bought your little beauty."

"I can't imagine where we could be going that could do justice to your car or how we amazing we look," Anna said. She smoothed her hands over the plush seats and inhaled the smell of leather.

"Actually, I meant to ask you about that. How do you

feel about flying?"

"I'm amicable to the idea," Anna said, raising her eyebrow in question. "Why?"

"You'll see," Dylan said, speeding across the city line. "I think we'll leave Paradise behind for tonight."

## CHAPTER ELEVEN

"This is so cool," Anna said, looking down at the clouds below. "I had no idea you owned your own plane."

"Let's just say that business has been good over the years."

"Ah, yes. You said you haven't always worked in Paradise. What did you do before you opened Maguire Homes?"

"Well, you might have heard of a little business called TexAmerica Real Estate?"

"You own TexAmerica?" Anna asked in awe. TexAmerica was the biggest name in Real Estate in the southwest.

"No, I used to own TexAmerica. Well, Mitchell and I owned it together, and then we sold it for a lot of money.

I decided I liked the more hands on approach to the business. He poured two flutes of champagne and handed her one.

"Mitchell and I met in college, and we both knew exactly what we wanted to do with our lives. He majored in architecture and I majored in Engineering, and when we graduated we opened TexAmerica and hired a few hungry Real Estate agents. Most of them aren't hungry anymore. We got tired of the city life, sold the business and moved to Paradise."

He conveniently left out the series of events that had led to their escape. Denise, his ex-wife, had left him for a doctor when she'd thought the company was going to go belly up. She was cutting her losses she'd told him in the divorce hearing. Then Mitchell's wife had died in a horrible car crash. Both of them were looking for a way to get out.

"Wow, so you're filthy rich," Anna said.

"Pretty much. I hope that's not too much of a turnoff."

"I won't hold it against you if you don't hold it against me," she said, toasting him with her full glass.

"It's a deal. I took the liberty of having an overnight bag prepared for you. Mel was more than willing to help."

"Ah, bless her," Anna said. "I can only imagine the

gossip tomorrow if I returned in the same dress I left in. Where are we going, by the way?"

"No place too far. We should be landing in Dallas in about thirty minutes. We have plenty of time to check into the hotel and freshen up before dinner. Now why are you sitting so far away from me?" he said, patting his lap playfully.

"Do you have any idea how long it took me to get ready for tonight? I don't want to check into a hotel looking like I just rolled out of bed," Anna said, taking his hand and sitting across his lap as he directed her.

"I promise not to muss you up too much," Dylan said, biting the back of her neck.

Anna shivered at the touch of his lips and teeth against her. It had been so long since she'd felt his touch and if she was honest with herself, she'd missed him terribly in the time she'd been away.

"I've missed you," he said, echoing her thoughts. He traced his fingers lightly along the outline of her body. "And I've wanted you every day that you've been gone."

"Mmm. . ." Anna moaned as she felt the zipper of her dress slide down slowly. "What about the pilot?" she asked, worried that he'd come out of the cockpit and find them.

"His orders are to stay in the cabin and leave us our

privacy, but we don't have long before we land." He helped her stand and slipped the column of turquoise silk to her feet. "Oh my God. You have the most amazing underwear I've ever seen."

"You can thank Mel for that, too. She picked it all out for me."

"Remind me to buy her something nice." He stood up behind her and removed his tie and shirt, never taking his eyes of her scantily clad body. She looked like an underwear model with her toned body and high heels.

"I can't believe you hid this body under all those ugly clothes. Think of all the months we've wasted."

"I shudder to think," she said, unable to take her eyes off his own fantastic form. It was the first time she was able to really see his body in the light. Their previous time together had been fast and furious, lust and heat and fulfillment found by groping in the dark.

"Yummy," Anna said, licking her lips. "You're not too shabby yourself."

Dylan brought her close, so their bodies barely touched, and kissed her passionately, their lips melding in perfect accord. The intensity grew and the kiss became softer, slower, deeper, until he was sure he'd die with the taste of her on his lips.

Anna slipped her finger just under the edge of his

slacks, touching the sensitive skin around his middle. She unhooked them so they pooled around his feet, and she found him ready for her, heavy with arousal.

"I need you," she said, kissing the underside of his jaw. She hitched herself up and wrapped her legs tightly around his waist. The only thing separating them was the thin swatch of lace that covered her mound. Her hands skimmed up and down his back, and her nails bit into his shoulders as she felt her bra slip away, leaving her totally bare before him.

Dylan kissed her again, this time hotter and harder than before, branding her with every stroke of his tongue. The scent of her was everywhere, clouding his mind with the haze of lilac and desire.

The sun was setting and the last rays of light reflected off her golden skin. He couldn't help but kiss his way down to her breast and sample the sweetness there. He trailed his fingers over the arch of her back as she leaned across his arm, her legs still wrapped around him firmly, and he devoured the sensitive flesh.

"You are so beautiful," he said as the sun's final light illuminated her body. He lifted her higher so she arched over the back of a leather recliner on the private jet, and he ran his fingers just inside of the black lace panties she wore.

He left the soft flesh of her breast and nuzzled his way down to the taut skin of her belly, making her muscles quiver, and then jump as his lips closed over the thin lace.

"Oh, God. . ." Anna moaned out at the feel of the wet heat of his mouth against her core. "Mmm. . ."

Dylan moved her to the chaise lounge and laid her down gently. He removed her panties and looked at the petals before him, glistening with need and desire for him. He placed his palm over her heat and watched as her eyes clouded with surprise as he drove her up to a fierce peak.

He replaced his palm with the tip of his tongue and stroked her gently, watching as she went up in flames again, sobbing out his name until she went limp with pleasure.

He'd never wanted another woman as much as he wanted Anna, and now he knew he never would. He was determined for her need to be as fierce as his own, for her love to mirror his. Love. There was that word again. He was tired of fighting it.

"I need to touch you," Anna said, reversing their roles. She pushed him over so she rose above him and devoured him with her mouth and hands, desperate to feel him against her.

"Let me. Let me touch you," she begged desperately.

He was so hard beneath her touch—hard and hot

enough to set them both ablaze with one embrace. She skimmed her mouth down his body with wet kisses and then finally took him in her mouth.

The breath hissed out of his lungs at the feel of her mouth circling him, stroking him until he knew he wouldn't last a minute longer with any more of her sweet torment.

"God...stop," he begged. "I won't last."

She needed to be joined with him, more than she'd ever needed anything. She straddled his lean hips and prepared to take him to the hilt.

"Not yet," he said as he flipped their positions once again, rolling her onto her stomach. "I want to feel you under me."

"God. Please. Please Now," she yelled. She was mad with want, and she felt the control leave her body as she hurtled toward insanity. She gripped the head of the chaise in a fierce grip as he bit the back of her neck in passion, like a stallion ready to mount his mare.

"Now," he echoed as he plunged into her.

He seized her hips in a hard grasp and rode her hard, spurred on by the little cries she made in the back of her throat. He felt her close around him in a tight grip, her silky sheath made especially for him, and cry out a scream of ecstasy in her release.

"More," Dylan said as he turned her back over to face him.

He slipped back into her easily, her flesh swollen and clasping him tighter in its embrace. She arched into him, the rise and fall of their bodies like a sinuous dance, as flesh met flesh. He watched her turquoise eyes as they clouded over with pleasure, and he hoped with all his heart it was love he saw shining in their depths.

She pulled him to her tightly, gripping fiercely with her arms and thighs, as she came in a violent climax that left her shattered.

"Dylan."

The sound of his name coming from her lips brought forth his own climax, and he emptied himself inside of her with the promise to love her forever spoken from his lips.

Dylan felt her stiffen beneath him and knew he'd spoken the words from his heart aloud. He wasn't about to take them back though. They were spared from having to talk about it by the captain coming over the intercom announcing they'd be landing in the next few minutes.

Dylan got up slowly on shaky legs and helped Anna into an upright position. He watched her as she kept her gaze down and gathered up her clothes.

"I'm going to clean up in the restroom and get myself

put back together," she told him, never making eye contact and closing herself in the bathroom.

He pulled on his clothes, thoughts weighing heavily in his mind. This wasn't the way he'd imagined love between two people. He didn't really have anything to compare to since his first marriage had never come close to experiencing the emotion. But Anna was different. He loved her, and the pain piercing his chest told him it was real because surely if it was only lust it wouldn't make him feel as if his heart had been ripped out when she didn't reciprocate the feelings.

He sat down in his seat and downed the untouched glass of champagne he'd poured Anna earlier. The plane touched down in Dallas with little fuss and he grabbed both of their bags and headed to the bathroom door.

"Are you ready?" he yelled through the closed door. He felt they were miles apart instead of mere inches. He'd been taking one step forward and threes steps back since the beginning of their relationship.

Anna stepped out of the restroom with a forced smile plastered on her face, but her eyes were wary and a little scared. "I'm ready when you are."

Dylan seriously doubted the statement, but followed her out of the plane and into the waiting car anyway.

## CHAPTER TWELVE

The Mansion on Turtle Creek was a five star hotel and restaurant Dylan had frequented often when he'd lived in the city, for business and for pleasure, and he'd wanted to give Anna a memorable experience on their impromptu trip. So far, memorable was definitely an apt description.

"Good evening Mr. Maguire." The bellman greeted Dylan like an old friend and took the two bags from the trunk of the rental car.

"Nice to see you again, Maurice. It's been a while," Dylan said, discreetly palming a tip into his hand.

Anna looked at the hotel in wonder. It was perfect. Small and tucked away in its own private forest, the running water of its famous creek a trickle in the background. She followed Dylan up to their suite and kept silent, unsure of what she could possibly say. She felt empty and ashamed that she'd let herself fall in love with a man who wasn't capable of loving her for an eternity.

She'd heard the words she was thinking slip through his lips, but she'd also seen the expression of regret as soon as he'd said them. She knew logically that men said things they wouldn't normally in the heat of the moment, but it didn't make the want to hear them or the need to believe them any less painful.

Dylan had probably said those words to dozens of women over the years. Why should she be the exception? In fact, why should she be the one to spill her guts and take a chance on love when it was all just a word game to him? She was the one who had the most to lose. Love wasn't something that came easily to her. She knew *she* loved Dylan, but she was still afraid of what it meant. And now her fear was doubled because what would happen when he realized he didn't really love her back?

She walked into the suite and headed over to the desk. She ignored their private view of the creek that could be seen perfectly from the lake sized, four-poster bed that sat in the middle of the room. She'd tackle the bed issue later. The room was spacious and open, but she felt as if the walls were closing in on her with Dylan standing mere feet away.

"I need to make some business calls before all the stores close for the night," Anna said, thinking of the first excuse that came to mind so she could avoid being alone with him a little longer.

"Fine," Dylan said, his voice flat. "I'm going to head down to the bar for a drink. Our reservation is at seven thirty."

He closed the door behind him with a controlled effort Anna had to admire. He was angry with her, but she should be the one who was angry.

She walked out onto the balcony, her phone calls forgotten, and lost herself in thought. They'd have to come to an understanding before the night was over. Her heart was too vulnerable to make love to him again without letting him know her feelings.

She looked over her shoulder at the bed that beckoned lovers by the sight of it. Things were bound to get more difficult as the night went on.


Dylan nursed his Scotch on the rocks as he waited for Anna to walk into the bar. What had he been thinking, leaving himself wide open for rejection, again.

He heard the conversation in the bar dim and knew Anna had walked into the room. He had the same reaction every time he saw her. She was beautiful, but she was sweet and kind and funny. The complete package. She made him laugh and she made him want with an intensity that frightened him at times.

He turned in his seat and watched her make her way towards him, turning every male eye in her direction. Her eyes were locked to his, and she never noticed the other men's stares.

"Are you ready for dinner?" she asked.

"I've been looking forward to it all day," he said, matching her strained smile with one of his own.

He put his hand in the small of her back and led her to the dining area, scowling in the direction of a few men whose gazes lingered a little too long.

"How about some champagne?" Dylan asked as if they were celebrating. The steward took the order and scurried off to procure their best bottle.

"So," Dylan said, finally getting the eye contact he'd been waiting for. "How long are you going to pretend I didn't say it?"

The color slowly drained from Anna's face. "I don't know what you mean," she said, busying herself by straightening the silverware in front of her.

"You know exactly what I mean. I want to know why you won't acknowledge it and why you're treating me like a stranger."

"I just don't think it's significant."

"You don't think me telling you I love you is significant?" Dylan asked. People were beginning to turn and stare, the volume of his voice a little louder than necessary.

"Ssh. . ." Anna said, mortified. "I don't think it's significant because I'm sure it's a term you use rather loosely with all of the women you sleep with."

Now it was Dylan's color that drained, leaving his pallor ashen with anger. "I noticed that you didn't come to me a virgin. Why do you get to throw my past in my face? What if I told you the women from my past are meaningless because the only woman I want from now on is you? Do you think I'm so incapable of change?"

Anna kept silent at his outburst. She found it hard to believe that he'd only want her from now on, but he was right about throwing his past in his face. "I apologize for what I said."

"You're sorry for saying it to my face. That doesn't mean you're not still thinking it. That word has never left my mouth, not to any other woman I've ever been with, not even to my ex-wife. It's a word that scares the shit out of me every time I hear it, but you think it's insignificant?"

Anna was shocked by Dylan's confession. She had no idea that he'd been serious in his declaration, and she was about to tell him so when he continued talking.

"I got married the first time because my ex-wife told

me she was pregnant. That was the only reason. She lied about the baby and the little spark of love I felt for that baby fizzled, and hate for her took up that space in my soul. I was relieved when she walked out the door and into her new lover's Lexus. I have never wanted a woman the way I want you, and I sure as hell have never loved a woman the way I love you. Though God knows why because the way you keep running away from me would probably discourage a lesser man."

Their dinner was served without fanfare, the silence and tension at the table so thick it could be cut with a knife. The waiters approached their table like it was wired to explosives.

"Do you know what my reaction was when you told me today that you could be pregnant?" Dylan asked. "I didn't realize it at the time because I was shocked and scared, but my overall gut feeling was joy because what better way to celebrate how much I love you than with a child."

Anna didn't know what to say, so she kept silent. Her own insecurities were bringing out the only defense mechanism she had. Anger. It was building inside her, and she knew it would come to a head before too long. She picked at the buttery lobster that sat in front of her, unable to enjoy its taste.

"You know what I think?" Dylan asked. "I think you're the one with the issues here. I've faced my fears and laid my heart open for you, but you're still hiding from yourself and your own fears. What are you so afraid of?"

"What's there *not* to be afraid of?" she asked, uncaring they were in the middle of a crowded restaurant and everyone was more interested in their conversation than the food in front of them. They probably would have been escorted out if Dylan hadn't been such a valued guest.

"What in the world makes you think I'd want to risk loving you, only to lose you or watch you walk away in the end? I watched my father fall to pieces after my mother died. He has never been the same, only half the man he could be. Do you think I've never dreamed of being in love? That I want to spend my life alone? What person would? But can I lay open my heart and soul to you, and not be a broken and bitter person when you decided to move on to your next conquest. I don't know if I can. And I don't know if it's worth the risk."

"Sometimes you have to put everything on faith when it's something this important. It's not just about love, but the other things that go with it, like trust. When I say I love you, it's a promise, not a convenience. These are your hang ups that you're going to have to overcome. All I can do is love you."

Tears were streaming down Anna's cheeks. Confusion and hurt clouded her mind and all she wanted was to hide in the shell she'd developed so many years before. She brushed the tears away quickly as the check was brought, and as soon as Dylan signed his name she stood and headed towards the elevators.

Dylan followed at a slower pace behind her, but his eyes stayed glued to her retreating form. She was distancing herself from him again, but he wasn't going to let her get away with it this time.

The elevator ride was made in strained silence until the other passengers departed on their own floors.

"After you," Dylan said sarcastically as he opened the suite door for her.

Anna was just about to suggest that she sleep on the pull out couch in the sitting room when Dylan pulled her into his arms.

"Do you honestly think I'm going to leave you alone tonight and let you sulk?" Dylan asked, pushing her against the wall.

The door to the room slammed with such finality she was sure she'd never be able to escape. The coolness of the wall at her back warred with the heat of Dylan's body as it pressed forcefully against her.

"The last thing I'm going to do is give you a chance to run."

He brought his mouth to her own in a brutal kiss, a kiss to remind her who she was with and who wanted her.

She moaned into his mouth even though her hands pushed him away. Every nerve in Anna's body hummed at the feel of his lips touching her skin. But it was wrong. There was too much at stake to make love like neither one of them had any sense left.

"Stop Dylan," she begged. "This isn't the way to do this. There are too many things to sort out."

"It's exactly the way to do this. I'm about to make you face your fears head on."

His lips roamed over her face, to the tender spot just below her jaw and then to the pulse in her neck. He bit and suckled making her squirm with pleasure. The want never dimmed when she was in his arms. All the fear and doubt fled as he felt how her body molded to his perfectly.

"No, don't do this," she said, even as her traitorous arms pulled him closer.

Starving to be inside her, though it had only been hours since their last joining, he pushed her dress up around her waist and plunged his fingers inside of her waiting heat. His need was fierce, the urge to possess overwhelming any gentleness he might have had.

He could hear her rapid breathing as he took her up, peak after peak. He slid his tongue over her quivering skin until he captured her breast. The prick of his teeth against her sensitive flesh sent her erratic pulse scattering.

He was wild with want, with a restrained violence that Anna had never seen before. And the hunger she felt leaping in her own body was primal in its need to mate with this man. It was life and death, good and evil, joy and hate all rolled into one.

Anna grabbed frantically at the clothes still covering his body. She pulled at his shirt until buttons started to fly, and she fumbled at the snap on his trousers. His fingers bit into the delicate flesh at her hips as he kept her anchored between his body and the wall, and he groaned as he felt her hands grasp his rigid cock in her hand. He fused his mouth to hers once again and pushed against her opening until he felt the wet heat envelop him fully.

He thought briefly about the condoms in his bag and knew he should stop to get them, but he couldn't do it. The feel of her around him was too great, and a little voice in his head told him he was desperate enough for Anna to see his love that he wasn't above getting her pregnant to get through to her.

He began to rock against her, slowly at first, then faster, faster until he was driven way past the point of reason. The only thing in the world at that moment was her. Only her. He felt her tighten around him and shudder in his arms. All he could do was follow in his own release.

He leaned against her, their blood and heartbeats cooling along with the sheen of sweat that lightly coated their bodies.

"This doesn't change anything," Anna said.

Dylan found the energy to raise his head and look into her eyes. The tears coursing down her cheeks caused his heart to contract, but he understood her fear because it used to be his own.

"It changes everything," he said. He carried her over to the bed, still intimately joined, and laid her on the soft down quilts. He smoothed the tears from her cheeks and kissed them gently.

Her eyes were wide and luminous as he began to move inside her slowly, tenderly. This wasn't the furious coupling they'd shared before but something deeper, more intimate. It was a dance, give and take, swaying bodies and gentle moonlight.

"I love you," he said as the tempo quickened and soft sighs became urgent moans.

"Look at me," Dylan demanded when Anna closed her eyes to block the feelings she saw in his own. It was too much, too powerful for her to stand. She did love him, and when he was in her arms like this she couldn't remember why she needed to resist him.

"I love you," he said again, and crushed his mouth to hers.

His need for her didn't diminish as the night grew

longer. And her passion met his own, even when he could tell she was exhausted.

The shadowy light of dawn was just beginning to glow pearly gray when he turned her to her back and slipped inside her. She was still half asleep, but her body welcomed him. He propped her legs over his arms and moved slowly, in and out, from the base of his cock to the very tip.

"Do you want me to stop?" he asked as her eyes fluttered open to meet his gaze.

"No. Don't stop. Not ever."

"Good." He leaned down and kissed her softly, entwining his tongue with hers in a lazy dance. And then he nipped sharply at her bottom lip, causing her to gasp with pleasure. "I told you we'd explore the desire you seem to have for a little pain."

He kept his thrusts steady as he moved his mouth down to her breasts. Her nipples were tight buds, the color of ripe cherries, just begging for his mouth to find them. He laved one with his tongue before giving it a sharp bite with his teeth. Her pussy spasmed around his cock, and he groaned at pleasure. He gave the same attention to the other and felt his balls draw tighter with every spasm she had.

He pulled out of her before he spent himself too quickly and turned her to her stomach. He propped pillows beneath her, so her ass was put on display before him. He entered her from behind, loving the way he disappeared inside of her. She was so wet, and he used his fingers to spread her juices higher, dipping his finger into the tight bud of her anus.

"Mmm," she moaned.

"Do you like that?" Dylan asked, slipping two fingers inside the tight hole as he continued his assault on her pussy with his cock.

"Yessssss. It feels so good."

He stretched his fingers and lubricated her with her own cream. Sweat beaded on his brow, and his muscles strained with the effort to not spend himself too soon. He wanted his cock in her ass with a ferocity that made him shake. It was an intimacy that would bring them closer together than ever before.

"Do you want me to fuck you here?" he whispered in her ear, nipping at the lobe. His other hand was beneath her rubbing her clitoris in slow circles while his cock was buried inside her and his fingers moved in and out of her ass.

"Oh, God. I can't take it anymore. It's too much."

"There's no such thing as too much pleasure, Anna. Just like there's no such thing as too much love. If I take you in your ass it means you belong to me. And only me.

Is that what you want?" He emphasized the question by flicking her clit until she hung just on the edge of orgasm.

"Yes, please. Just fuck me."

"I want to hear you say you belong to me. Say it, and I'll give you what you want."

Her breath heaved in and out of her chest, and her body trembled with need. Her voice choked out a sob when she answered. "I belong to you, Dylan. Only you."

Dylan roared with triumph and pulled out of her dripping pussy, moving to the small hole he'd stretched to accommodate his size. He pushed his bulbous head past the tight entrance, gritting his teeth at the pleasure that gathered in his balls. Once his head slipped past the tight ring, he slid all the way to the hilt. His hands grabbed her hips and he began thrusting.

Her cries of rapture couldn't drown out his own. He'd never felt anything like this before. It was as if they were as close as two people could ever be. Heart to heart. Soul to soul. He pulled her up so her back rested against his chest and she sat partially on his knees. He strummed her clit with his fingers and plucked at her nipples. And when she tightened around him in a vise so tight he thought he'd lose consciousness, he buried his face in her neck and let his balls empty into her waiting depths.

Dylan pulled out of her and collapsed on top of her. He pulled her into his arms. "I love you, Anna." But the words went unheard because she was already asleep.

## CHAPTER THIRTEEN

"Well, what do you think?" Dylan asked Mitchell as he showed him the 2-carat brilliant diamond ring nestled in a little blue box.

"I think you're an idiot. Do you remember when we used to come to this place everyday, sit down at our desks and work to meet our deadlines? When can we start doing that again?" Mitchell asked, rubbing his throbbing temples.

"So. . .does that mean you think she won't like it?"

"I think you've lost your mind, but that's just me," he said throwing his arms up in the air in defeat. There was no talking Dylan out of something once he'd made up his mind. "I'm not sure why you felt you needed to buy an engagement ring when the last time you saw each other you gave her an ultimatum and she walked out of your life. Again."

"I didn't give her an ultimatum. Exactly. I just told her I loved her and that she needed to do some serious soul searching. She claims she loves me, but she doesn't trust me to be able to love her back. Then I told her I wanted to spend the rest of my life with her, but I wouldn't keep making a fool of myself over someone who didn't feel I was worth loving. And then she ran," Dylan said undeterred. "Again."

Their romantic getaway hadn't worked out exactly as he'd planned. They'd turned to each other over and over again in the darkness of the night, and he'd shown her the depth of his love in every possible way.

But when the morning had come, she'd been unable to trust he'd been sincere, and he didn't have the heart to push her any more. She'd looked defeated and tired. He'd decided the best thing to do was let nature take its course and leave her alone.

The flight back to Paradise had been strained and silent until he'd dropped her off at her house. Now that he had a chance to think about it, he guessed he had given her an ultimatum. That had been two weeks ago, and he still hadn't seen her around town. Absence did make the heart grow fonder. He hoped she felt the same way.

"And that conversation gave you the confidence you needed to buy an engagement ring equal to some people's yearly salaries?"

"No, but I have confidence in Anna. I know she loves me, she just has to get over this fear of not being able to control what happens in the future and learn to trust me a little."

"I saw her this morning," Mitchell mentioned casually. "I took her through the house. She seemed pleased with the progress."

"How'd she look?"

"She looked sad. I told her I missed seeing her smile, and then I told her you were miserable and never let me get any work done anymore, so would she please come to her senses and give you a break. And then I kissed her passionately and made her forget all about you."

"In your dreams," Dylan said, laughing.

"And they were damn good dreams too, my friend. Now can we please get back to work? I'd like to be able to take my yearly vacation to Cancun. The women so look forward to my visits."

"I bet," Dylan said. "Why don't you ask Mel to go with you? I bet the women would start looking forward to her visits too."

"Shut up. Isn't that the dumbest thing you've ever heard? She's no more a lesbian than I am, but for some reason she's scared to death of me.

"Well, you're not as good looking as I am. And I hear there are other parts that don't measure up as well."

They were both laughing uproariously when Janet knocked on the door and walked in without waiting for an answer. She smiled at their antics, used to the relaxed atmosphere around the office.

"I see the two of you have already finished the contracts I put on your desk this morning," she said, glancing at the untouched folders that lay on Mitchell's desk.

"Oh, yeah," Dylan lied smoothly. "We're all caught up."

"Good, because I brought in a few more for you to go over. They need to be finished this afternoon," she said smirking at their grimaces. She was used to keeping her boys in line, and she knew just what buttons to push to get the results she wanted. You couldn't be an executive secretary and not know how to manipulate the people that worked there.

"Fine, fine. We'll get them done today. Looks like we'll have to postpone our trip to Shiney's until later tonight Mitchell."

"Whatever, as long as you're the one buying," Mitchell said, already reading the contracts.

"Oh, and the new contractor you hired stopped by

earlier to pick up a couple of the new clients you don't have room for. He went out to the sites to get a better feel for what the clients want. I have to say, Dylan, you have great taste in men. He is something scrumptious to look at," Janet said, winking at a laughing Mitchell.

"I didn't hire him because he looked scrumptious, as you put it," Dylan said peeved. "I hired him because he's damn good at his job. I got lucky luring him away from the firm he was at before."

"Hey, let me ask you something," Dylan said before she could walk out of the room. "What do you think about this?" he said, pulling the ring out of his pocket for her to see.

"Why Dylan, I didn't know that you cared," Janet said, batting her eyelashes and drawing a laugh.

"No, I mean, as a woman, is this something you'd like?" Dylan asked, a little unsure of himself.

"It's beautiful. Any woman would love that. It's huge and it's sparkly, what more could you ask for? I didn't know you were thinking of getting engaged."

"I bought it for Anna."

"I didn't think the two of you were seeing each other any more," Janet said, confused.

"Thank you," Mitchell said applauding. "Everybody sees the pattern except for you buddy."

"She just needed some time off to think," Dylan said, looking at the ring once more before putting it back in his pocket. "She'll come to her senses soon enough."

They all watched in slow motion as Janet's bracelet flew off her wrist when she lifted her arm to touch the ring. The loose clasp made it easy to come off, and she was always surprised she hadn't lost it before now.

"Hey, you're welcome to come to Shiney's with us tonight if you want?" he told her. He picked up the silver bracelet that always seemed to come unfastened and handed it back to her.

"Thanks, but no thanks. I've got a hot date tonight, and I'm expecting fireworks."

"She really needs to get that bracelet fixed," Dylan said, putting the ring back in his pocket and looking at the stack of files in front of him.

"Well, what do you think?" Anna asked Mel as she twirled around.

"Of the dress or of the idea?" Mel asked.

"Both."

"Well, I have to say from a lesbian's perspective, the dress is hot. As far as the plan goes, I think you're an idiot."

"Great!" Anna said, admiring herself in the mirror. The dress was pale blue and form-fitting, held up only by thin rhinestone spaghetti straps. She needed to look her best for what she had planned.

"I've got to put myself out on a ledge if this is going to work. It's my turn to put pride aside. I've finally come to my senses."

"I never would have guessed," Mel said sarcastically.

"I've been completely unreasonable. Dylan loves me, and I threw it back in his face. I'm going to have to face my fears and put my trust in him."

"Hello. . .That's what I've been telling you from the beginning."

"I know, but it was something I had to figure out on my own. It was a mindset I'd ingrained since my mom died, and old habits are hard to break. But I'm going to knock his socks off tonight."

"I think he'll definitely be surprised, and I think you're father is going to kill you. But maybe people will stop talking about me."

"I could probably dance naked in the Towne Square and people would still talk about you," Anna said, laughing. "Lesbians are hard to come by in Paradise."

"What was I thinking?" Mel asked.

"I don't know, because it didn't work. Mitchell seems determined to make you admit that you like men."

"Yeah, he's getting pretty serious about it, almost like it's a contest of wills. Have you seen the new guy they hired earlier this week?"

"No. I didn't know they hired anyone."

"Mitchell told me they're getting too many clients to get the job done exactly the way they want it, so they're bringing in a new partner. I think he came from a firm in Houston. All I know is that he's not hard to look at. This could be it, Anna. This could be my one and only."

"You know the saying about how a watched pot never boils?" Anna asked.

"Yeah."

"Well, I think it works the same with love. I think it's supposed to hit you when you least expect it."

"Maybe, but that doesn't mean I'm not going to give it my best shot," she said, slightly deflated. "Do you really think you'll be able to go through with this tonight?"

"What's the worse that can happen?"

"That's what I'm afraid of.


Jack Hollis hung up the phone, his hand shaking

slightly at what the sheriff had told him. Anna had been getting threats for weeks and she hadn't said a word to him about it.

In fact, since she'd become her "new" self, she'd stopped talking to him about everything. He kept up with her life just like the rest of the town—through the grapevine.

He knew that she and Dylan had a pretty serious relationship going on, only Anna was the one too afraid to commit. He never would have seen that one coming if Mitchell hadn't told him that piece of news.

Sure Dylan liked to play the field, but Jack knew from the first moment he met the boy that he had a sense of honor about him. Dylan was just waiting for the right woman to come along and settle him down a bit. And Anna was that woman. Surely if she looked deep down inside of Dylan, she'd realize he was crazy about her.

Jack had faith in his daughter. She'd come to her senses when the time came. She was just as stubborn and head strong as her mother had been, and lord knew it had taken him months to wear her down until she'd finally agreed to marry him.

Now as far as the matter of threats went, he wasn't about to stand by and let some maniac endanger his daughter. He'd already lost one woman he'd loved. No, if Anna refused to be in Dylan's company then she had no choice but to stay in his.

He watched as Mel and Anna walked down the stairs, arm in arm, giggling over some foolish nonsense just like when they'd been teenagers.

"Well, well ladies. Don't you look lovely tonight," Jack said beaming at them.

Anna had finally talked Mel into pulling the big guns out in the hopes of dissuading the rumors currently floating around town. Maybe she'd get lucky and find the man of her dreams. Mel's outfit was a bright contrast compared to Anna's pastel blue, and matched her bubbling personality. The hot pink halter top and hip hugging Capri pants showed off her curvy figure.

"And where are the two of you off to looking so stunning?" Jack asked.

"We're on our way to Shiney's," Anna said as she grabbed her purse and bent to kiss him on the cheek.

"You know, girls," Jack said, "that sounds like a great idea. Would you mind if I joined you?"

He was thinking about the threats Anna had been getting and of her safety, so he didn't see the embarrassed expression flit across her face.

"Sure Mr. Hollis," Mel said, barely containing her laughter. She ignored Anna's imploring stare and gave her a wink instead. "This'll be fun."

"Yeah, fun," Anna muttered following close behind

them.

## CHAPTER FOURTEEN

Dylan and Mitchell settled themselves into a corner booth, nursing their beers and enjoying the live band that Shiney's always had on family nights and the weekends. The smoke filled interior was controlled chaos, an art form that had been successful for decades with waitresses dodging bodies and spilled drinks and whoever was tending bar keeping up with the piling orders.

They were somewhat secluded from the growing Thursday night crowd, preferring to observe instead of participate, and they looked over the menu in companionable silence.

"What'll it be boys?" Verna Shiney asked in her booming voice. Brian's mother ruled the roost in the Shiney household, and she'd been taking orders and filling drinks for many years.

"I think we'll both have the special tonight," Dylan answered. "I like the new band. I can actually hear conversations going on around me."

"I know what you mean. I couldn't hear anything in my left ear for a week after that band from last time. I hear you're still having a few lady problems," Verna said with a wink.

"I wouldn't call them problems exactly," Dylan said. "I just need to work on my persuasive techniques a little more. What do you say Verna, would you like to run away to Tahiti with me?"

"Oh, you rascal. If I was forty years younger I'd take you up on it. I wouldn't turn a fine specimen like you away. I have no idea what's wrong with Anna. I helped diaper that girl. It makes me want to give her a good smack in the head," she said, heading off back to the kitchen.

"Ah, that's what I love about small towns. Everybody knows your business."

"I'm glad I'm not in your shoes because that's exactly what I don't like about small towns. You notice no one ever talks about me," Mitchell said.

"That's because you're boring. Your lesbian girlfriend is more exciting than you are."

"Shut up. I think we've reached an understanding

these past weeks, since you and Anna have screwed up everyone else's schedule. We've become allies."

"So you're telling me you're not attracted to Mel?" Dylan asked with a disbelieving look on his face.

"Nope. She's not my type. She's got a great sense of humor and she's smart, but I'm just not attracted to her that way. All I want is for her to admit that she's attracted to the opposite sex."

"I'll bet you a thousand dollars that you make a move on her before the year is out," Dylan said.

"That would be completely inappropriate, and she'd kick my ass if she ever found out."

"Pussy," Dylan taunted. "Ten thousand."

"You're on," Mitchell said. "And I would like my payment in cash, so I don't have to declare it on my taxes if you don't mind."

"In your dreams. You've never been able to resist an attractive woman, and now that a bet's on the line she's going to be damn near irresistible."

"We'll just see about that," Mitchell said, confidant.

"What the hell's going on over there?" Dylan asked, trying to see around a group of people. The area had suddenly become quiet and the only sound was the music coming from the band.

"Well, speak of the devil," Dylan murmured with a smile on his face.

Mitchell turned around to see what Dylan was looking at and his jaw almost dropped to the floor. There was Mel, standing in the middle of the doorway, looking like he'd never seen her before.

Gone were the trendy clothes and funky hairstyle and in its place was a woman that could melt fire. The form-fitting outfit she wore accented all the curves he loved. Her lips were slicked the color of raspberries, and he had to restrain himself from wanting to taste them.

"That was the easiest ten grand I've ever made, my friend," Dylan said.

"The bet's not over yet," Mitchell said, his palms sweaty but his mind determined to win. "And besides, your own problem just walked in the door."

Dylan shot out of his chair in a flash and looked back towards the door, unmindful of the attention he'd drawn to himself.

Anna walked in directly behind Mel, dressed just as sexy, and leaned back to say something to her father. Great, Dylan thought, Jack would be with her tonight. He couldn't very well pull her into a soul-searching kiss while her father was standing three feet away.

"Shit," Dylan said.

"Exactly. You are screwed, not to mention how desperate you look. You're totally ruining the image we've been building for so many years."

"What can I say? I'm a one woman man from now on," he said, devouring the sight of Anna with his eyes. "What's she doing?"

"Looks like they're going to sit at the bar to me. What the hell is Mel doing talking to Brian Shiney?" Mitchell growled.

"Anna told me they've all been friends since grade school. They hang out all the time. In fact, I heard they were planning a trip to Las Vegas soon. They go every couple of years. Why, are you jealous?"

"Hell no," Mitchell said, seeing red at the thought of Mel taking a trip with anyone, "but that doesn't mean I think she should be traipsing around dressed like that and flirting with every man she sees.

"See there," Mitchell pointed, "See how she's hugging Walt Mooneyham."

Dylan burst into laughter at Mitchell's absurdity. "Walt Mooneyham is ninety-two years old. I don't think you have anything to worry about."

"I'm not worried. I just think she should have a care with how she advertises her wares."

"Do me a favor and mention that to her. I love it

when women kick your ass." Dylan's gaze wondered back to Anna, and his heart swelled with the love he felt for her. The need to get up and pull her into his arms was overwhelming.

"Oh my, God," Mitchell muttered. "That's Jeff."

Dylan looked toward the bar again and saw Jeff Zimmerman, their new partner, make a smooth move so he ended up right next to Mel.

Dylan started to laugh at the irony. "Looks like he's making some headway. And I believe Mel is returning the interest."

"Like hell she is," Mitchell muttered, then clamped his mouth shut when he realized he sounded like a jealous lover. "She's a grown woman. She can do whatever the hell she wants. But I think Jeff needs to be concentrating on the piles of work on his desk instead of making time with the local ladies."

Dylan ignored Mitchell's tirade and watched as Anna and Jack sat next to Mel on the barstools. It didn't take Verna Shiney long to make her way over to the trio. He held his breath as he watched Verna look in his direction, and he knew Anna was now aware of his presence.

She turned her head and their eyes met, held captive by the attraction that still shot like electricity between them. He smiled at her slowly, that devastating smile that melted her heart, and nodded in her direction.

Anna froze. She knew there was a chance he'd be here tonight, but she thought she'd have time to get her wits about her and do some deep breathing exercises before she had to jump off the deep end.

Dylan was confused by the look that came into Anna's eyes. She looked worried and a little bit hesitant. And if he hadn't missed his guess. . .nervous.

He watched her get up off her stool, and his heart pounded harder when he thought she was coming over to see him. But surprise showed on his face as he watched her walk in the opposite direction.

"She's giving you the cold shoulder, bud," Mitchell said, jabbing him in the ribs.

"No she's not, but she's up to something. That look she gave me was anything but cold."

"Look, now Anna's flirting with Brian. What's with that guy making time with our women," Mitchell asked.

"Our women?" Dylan asked.

"No, I didn't say that," Mitchell backpedaled. "I meant your woman."

"You are toast my friend. Here's to seeing if you can turn the lesbian to a lover of men and make me ten thousand dollars richer," Dylan said, lifting his beer.

He stopped with the beer halfway to his mouth when

he heard the band stop in mid chord and the sound of a spoon hitting a wine glass. He almost dropped his beer to the floor as he watched Anna climb up on the tall mahogany bar with Brian's help, her long legs exposed for everyone to see.

"Hello. . .When did this turn into Coyote Ugly?" Mitchell asked.

"Shut up. What's she doing?" Dylan stood up to get a better look and to run to the rescue if need be.

Anna looked around at the crowded room and knew she'd lost her mind. There was no turning back now. She'd already stopped the band and crawled on top of a six foot bar. There wasn't any chance in the world that she'd gone unseen and could just sit back down like nothing had happened.

"Could I have everyone's attention please?" she asked, though everyone's eyes were riveted in her direction, her father's included. *Sorry, Dad.*

This was a far cry from the girl she was two months ago. Panic seized her and she tried to relax before she ended up hyperventilating or worse, throwing up on some poor innocent patron. Mel gave her a thumb's up sign and she took a deep breath.

"Um, hi. Most of you have known me my whole life, and if you don't you've probably been talking about me the last few weeks anyway." She paused for the chuckles she heard in the crowd.

"I've got a few things to say. I need to say them in front of all of you but they're mostly directed to one person."

She scanned the crowd and found Dylan's eyes. He was standing towards the back of the room, the love shining so plainly on his face she didn't know how she could have possibly doubted him.

"As you all know, I've been seeing Dylan Maguire for several weeks now. Off and on," she added. "He's told me on several occasions that he loved me, but I didn't believe him. Why would someone like Dylan Maguire want me? I asked myself that question over and over again. I didn't trust him enough to think that he could be sincere."

Anna watched as Dylan started walking slowly to the front of the bar. "I've been selfish, and I almost let my past decide what my future should be." Tears coursed down her cheeks slowly. "I've finally come to the realization that my future is with Dylan, the good and the bad. I want to live my life with him and cherish every moment we have together. I want to apologize for the countless hurt that I've caused him over the past weeks, which I'm sure you've heard all about," she said with a watery laugh.

"But most importantly, I want to tell him that I love him, and hopefully, I haven't blown all my chances. I'd hate to have gotten up here and made a fool of myself for nothing. I promise I'll never run again and to stay with you as long as you want me."

Anna kept still and watched Dylan's reaction with bated breath. He stood with his hands in his pockets and rocked back on his heels slightly, his expression somber. The air in Shiney's was thick with anticipation, and several women blotted their damp cheeks with napkins.

"I guess I have something I need to say also," Dylan said as he walked up closer to Anna and held out his hand for her to grasp. He squeezed her shaking hand gently, knowing how much it had cost her to make a public announcement like that.

"I've spent many weeks chasing this woman around town, much to the delight of most everyone in this room. I never thought that love was something for me. It was something that happened to other people in other places. But then I met Anna, and from the first moment she walked into my life I knew she was the one for me, and I'm not afraid to say it scared the hell out of me."

He looked around the room to all the familiar faces that had become family to him over the past years and knew he'd never wanted to be anywhere else.

"So with that said, I'm also not afraid to do this here with all of you as witnesses. This way you don't have to hear it secondhand," he said winking at Douglas Howard.

He pulled the square blue box he'd been carrying

around in his pocket and held it up so everyone could see. He slipped the top off and let the black velvet ring box slip into his hand. He heard the gasps and sighs from everyone in the pub, but Anna's eyes stayed glued to his, love shining in their depths.

"Anna Hollis," he said. "To respond to your earlier statement, I'll want you forever. Not even the next fifty years will be enough to satisfy my love for you. I've loved you since the first moment I laid eyes on you. Will you marry me?"

He flipped the top of the ring box open and displayed the beautiful diamond sitting inside it. A token of his love forever. He watched the tears fall faster and her hand closed over her mouth in surprise. All she could do was nod her head in response to his question.

"I take that as a yes?" Dylan asked, slipping the ring on her finger.

The room erupted in applause as Dylan swung Anna down from the bar and enveloped her in his arms. Their lips found each other easily, and the passion ignited just as it always did when their bodies touched. He picked her up and swung her in a slow circle, never taking his lips from hers and feeling dizzy with love.

Dylan felt the hand on his shoulder just as he placed Anna back on the floor. He turned and saw Jack waiting for his attention, and he remembered he hadn't asked Jack's permission to marry Anna as he'd prepared to do when he'd first bought the ring.

He was surprised to see Jack stick out his hand. "Congratulations, son," Jack said, pulling them both into a hug. "You two sure were slow about this. I'm not going to live forever you know, and I would like some grandbabies before I get too old."

"We'll definitely take your request under consideration," Dylan said, smiling broadly. Hopefully, they'd already gotten started.

The crowd surged around them and he saw familiar faces congratulating them. What he didn't expect to see was Veronica lean over to hug Anna and wish them both well.

"Thank you, Veronica," Anna said graciously.

"Make sure you come by the boutique when you're shopping for your trousseau. I've got some things that will make your honeymoon interesting," she said with a wink.

Veronica went over to stand by Brian and ordered another drink. The two of them put their heads together so they could hear what the other was saying, and Dylan turned around in time to get hugs from both Mel and Mitchell.

"Geez, it's about time," Mel said. "Now I can go back to my boring life and actually get a little work done now and then."

"Amen," Mitchell said. "You two have worn me out. I think my vacation is going to come sooner rather than later."

Mitchell ushered Mel out of the crowd so they were isolated against a corner of the bar. It looked like he wasn't going to let Jeff put too many moves on Mel without him butting in to remind Mel that he'd been in her life first. There was no way Mitchell could win that bet. Mitchell was as fascinated with the complexity of Mel as he had been with Anna. The poor guy didn't have a chance.

Dylan led Anna to the door of Shiney's planning to make an escape so he could get her alone. He'd been dying to make love to her for weeks and now she was in his grasp forever. The crowd followed them out, cheering and wishing them well as they made their way to his truck.

The explosion rocked all the buildings that lined the Towne Square, and fire and metal shot into the air with the force of a canon.

Dylan threw Anna to the ground and covered her body with his own, others around them doing the same.

The heat was intense but mesmerizing at the same time. A twisted column of metal sat in the same place that Anna's car had been earlier in the evening. People were beginning to get up and watch the display, more exciting than the Fourth of July Parade they held every year.

"My car," Anna said, shock setting in. "My beautiful new car." Her eyes were dilated and her body was shaking with small tremors.

Dylan had never wanted to hurt anyone so bad in his entire life. Anna could very well have been in or near the car when the explosion went off. It was time to put an end to this.

"Some fireworks," Mitchell said, as he came up to stand next to Dylan.

"Yeah, and I think I know who's responsible," Dylan said angrily. "Anna, I want you to go home with your father and take Mel with you. I want you to promise me you'll stay inside until I get back. Don't go anywhere else," he demanded. "Do you promise?"

Anna was frightened enough to take his words to heart and not argue. He only had her safety in mind, but she wasn't too sure she was the only one in danger.

"Where are you going?" Anna asked, following him and Mitchell to his truck.

"I'm going to finish this. Tell Sheriff Haney to call me on my cell phone. Tell him I know who's behind this."

"Dylan," Anna yelled. "Be careful. The Willis house burning down was because of me. I don't think this person particularly cares who gets hurt. But I think they're determined to hurt someone. I don't want it to be you.

Dylan kissed her hard, and Anna watched as they drove away, her heart in her throat. She made the call to Sheriff Haney, but she hung up when she saw his cruiser already pulling up to the crime scene and went to tell him the news.

## CHAPTER FIFTEEN

Dylan followed his gut and sped through the old streets of Paradise, looking for the tiny house he'd only seen once before. He passed Mel's house on the right and Mitchell's a block further on the left, but still didn't recognize the one he was looking for.

"Come on, which one is it?" he asked, searching for any familiar signs.

"Look," Mitchell said and pointed to a house at the end of the block. The porch light came on, and someone was standing at the front door hurriedly locking up.

Dylan skidded to a stop in front of Janet's house, startling her into dropping her keys. She was dressed and ready to go out, and you never would have guessed by looking at her that she'd just blown up a hundred thousand dollar car.

"Hey, what are you guys doing here?" she asked, playing it cool and walking over to her car. "You've just caught me on my way out, so I won't be able to chat for long."

"I think you might just have to make the time," Dylan said.

Mitchell walked up to stand on the driver's side, blocking any escape she might have had.

"So tell me why you did it," Dylan said. "Anna's never done anything to hurt you, so why would you try to kill her?" He watched her eyes dilate quickly, and then she gained her composure, blanking her face of any expression.

"I don't know what you're talking about. Obviously you two have lost your minds. What, did Anna turn down your proposal and now you think I had something to do with it?"

"No, actually she didn't say no. She said yes. In fact, we made a public announcement. It was a shame you had to miss it."

"That's all very exciting, but what does this have to do with me?"

"You know, it's funny. After Anna told me she'd been run off the road, I tried to think of everyone possible that had a black car, and no one came to mind. Except the time you had to drive your mother's car to work when your's was in the shop. I wonder if we could match the skid marks at Paradise Crossing to that car."

He saw Janet's eyes widen in fear. "And then I began to go back and think of everything that had happened. The morning the Willis's house burned down, you were the only one that knew where I was going. Mitchell wasn't in the office yet, and you told me you'd give him the message. And then the notes, Janet. How very unoriginal. I can't believe you thought a note would keep Anna away from me."

"Of course I didn't think they would keep her away from you, but I needed to scare her enough that she'd question whether or not you were worth it."

"Why? You could have killed her. And I have to say, my first reaction after that car exploded was to do my own brand of murder. Consider yourself lucky."

"I never would have killed her. I knew exactly what I was doing. I was just going to scare her away from you. As to why... I've worked for you for four years, ever since you opened the office here, and yet you've never paid me the attention I deserved. I would have done anything for you, Anything!" she screamed.

"I never worried because I knew that you'd use your whores for pleasure, but you never attached yourself to any of them. You always came back to me. Until Anna. It was an insult to parade that dowdy, boring slut in front of me after everything I've done for you."

"Janet, I thought you were my friend."

"Just what every woman wants to hear, Dylan. The just friends speech."

"We could have been, Janet." Dylan paused when Sheriff Haney pulled up behind his truck and hopped out quickly. "But needless to say, I think I'm going to have to fire you. I love Anna, and her safety means everything to me. I'm sorry that I didn't know how you felt. But I can't change my feelings."

"Miss Porter," Sheriff Haney said. "Does this belong to you?" He held up a woven silver bracelet linked together with small diamonds. A bracelet that Dylan and Mitchell had seen on her wrist countless times.

Janet kept her mouth shut and continued staring holes into Dylan's chest.

"You know, the car explosion had the same MO as the fire at the Willis place. A match and a gas soaked rag that led to the fuel tank. I'm sure it wouldn't be any trouble at all to tie the two crimes together."

Janet turned her gaze to the sheriff, eyes hate filled and hard as granite.

"I believe you're going to have to come with me, Miss Porter." Sheriff Haney cuffed her wrists behind her back and led her to his cruiser. She never made a sound, but her stony silence spoke volumes.

"Life is always interesting in Paradise," Mitchell said, slapping Dylan on the back. "I can honestly say I've never been bored since moving here. Speaking of that, I believe you have a new fiancée who's waiting anxiously for you."

"No, I've been waiting for her my whole life. I just didn't know it."

# EPILOGUE

"Cut that out woman. Just once I'd like to make it to a nice soft bed before you start ravishing me."

"Excuse me," Anna said. "I believe it was you who picked the grass and the airplane and the wall and the creek behind the house and the. . ."

Dylan put his hand over her mouth and tried to look stern. "We haven't been married more than twenty-four hours and already you're back talking. You know you're supposed to be a submissive, obedient servant. I distinctly remember hearing that part in our vows."

"I must have been sleeping through that part," Anna said with a cheeky grin.

Dylan smacked her on the bottom and turned to look at the place they would be spending the next couple of days holed up in before they left for their honeymoon in

Hawaii. Anna's house was finished and it was spectacular. It already felt like more of a home than his ever had. Probably because Anna was there to share it with him.

"Are you sure you don't mind living here?" Anna asked. "I hate for you to put your house on the market if you don't want to."

"Anna, that house was just a place to live. It didn't mean anything to me. This house was the start of our whole relationship. I never want to live anywhere else."

They looked at the beautiful cottage surrounded by trees and a creek, a water wheel attached to the side of the house made it seem as if it came out of a fairytale. Its size was deceptive, for inside they had all the room they'd ever need, including the houseful of children they'd already started on.

He hoped the town wouldn't talk for too long about Anna giving birth only seven months after their wedding night, but he couldn't have been more excited to start their family.

Dylan swooped Anna up in his arms, the feel of her snug against him sending jolts through his body. He never tired of the feeling. "You know, the bed is an awfully long way from here, and I hear it's not good for expectant mothers to be on their feet for long periods of time."

"Well it just so happens I prepared for your lust crazed ideas," Anna said, nodding her head in the direction of the trees.

Dylan burst into laughter as he saw the sleeping bag nestled in a pile of leaves under a big oak tree. "That's more like it. I'd hate to waste any valuable time by walking all the way to the bedroom."

"You know I love you, Anna," he said, laying her gently on the ground.

"Show me," she said, opening her arms to welcome the delicious weight of his body against hers.

And he did.

## ABOUT THE AUTHOR

Liliana Hart is the pseudonym for an author of more than a dozen books. She lives in Texas with her husband and cats, and loves to be contacted by readers.

Connect with me online:

http://twitter.com/Liliana_Hart

http://facebook.com/LilianaHart

My Blog: http://lilianahart.blogspot.com

Made in the USA
San Bernardino, CA
07 November 2012